Kylie's hand pressed to her belly, and she was so very grateful for her unborn child.

Alex's child.

Whenever she looked at Brock and felt things she shouldn't feel, all she had to do was think about her baby. It was hard enough for one man to accept another's offspring. In Brock's case, it would be impossible. Whenever he looked at her, he probably thought about his half brother, Alex—the younger son, the one their father had loved.

How could she have such mixed feelings about all of it? How could she be grieving for Alex, but when Brock walked into the room she felt...*touched* in some way? Touched by an excitement, an electricity, a bond that had begun when she was seventeen and had never ended.

Had she loved Alex? Yes, she had. But she had to admit, Brock had always affected her...had always made her heart skip faster.

Dear Reader,

When I connect with someone either in friendship or in love, those bonds are lasting. My husband and I have been married thirty-five years. At our first meeting, did I know we'd be committed to each other for a lifetime? I feel I did. And he did, too. After a few months of dating, we certainly did. We had the same values, goals and dreams.

The hero and heroine in *Expecting His Brother's Baby* met when Kylie was seventeen. Was she too young to fall in love? Although she buried her feelings for Brock, the roots stayed strong. But so many obstacles blocked their connection.

Can love conquer all?

I believe true love can.

All my best,

Karen Rose Smith

EXPECTING HIS BROTHER'S BABY

KAREN ROSE SMITH

Silhouette

SPECIAL EDITION

Published by Silhouette Books

America's Publisher of Contemporary Romance

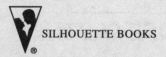 SILHOUETTE BOOKS

ISBN-13: 978-0-373-24779-0
ISBN-10:   0-373-24779-6

EXPECTING HIS BROTHER'S BABY

Books by Karen Rose Smith

Silhouette Special Edition

Abigail and Mistletoe #930
The Sheriff's Proposal #1074
His Little Girl's Laughter #1426
Expecting the CEO's Baby #1535
Their Baby Bond #1588
Take a Chance on Me #1599
Which Child Is Mine? #1655
Cabin Fever #1682
Custody for Two #1753
The Baby Trail #1767
Expecting His Brother's Baby #1779

Silhouette Books

The Fortunes of Texas
Marry in Haste...

Logan's Legacy
A Precious Gift

The Fortunes of Texas: Reunion
The Good Doctor

Signature Select

Secret Admirer
"Dream Marriage"

From Here to Maternity
"Promoted to Mom"

KAREN ROSE SMITH

read Zane Grey when she was in grade school, and she loved his books. She also had a crush on Roy Rogers and especially his palomino, Trigger! Around horses as a child, she found them fascinating and intuitive. Her BABY BONDS series set in Wyoming sprang from childhood wishes and adult dreams. When an acquaintance adopted two of the wild mustangs from the western rangelands and invited Karen to visit them, plotlines weren't far behind. For more background on the books in the series as well as photos and info about the wild mustangs, stop by Karen's Web site at www.karenrosesmith.com or write to her at P.O. Box 1545, Hanover, PA 17331.

Thanks to Gale Jacobs, who invited me to visit her adopted mustangs and learn their stories.

With appreciation to Francee and Dick Shaulles. Thanks for opening your home and ranch to us. Your family embodies the meaning of ranch life. We'll never forget our visit.

With appreciation to Ken Martin, who knows and understands the mustangs so well. Grey Face and his band had to be part of this book.

For information about wild mustangs, visit www.wildhorsepreservation.com. For adoption information go to www.wildhorseandburro.blm.gov.

Prologue

Wild Horse Junction, Wyoming

Kylie Warner didn't often compare herself to other women. She'd been a tomboy all her life, more comfortable on a horse than anywhere else. Function, rather than fashion, had always directed her clothing choice. But meeting this pert and sexily dressed waitress from Clementine's—Wild Horse Junction's watering hole—Kylie felt as if she'd let herself go. With her straight blond hair drawn back in a ponytail and her parka fitting snugly over her maternity outfit, she wondered what had happened to her sense of womanly pride since Alex died.

"I'm Trish," the waitress said with a smile that looked more forced than genuine. "We can use the boss's office. He went home for dinner."

When Trish had called Kylie, she'd said she wanted to talk about boarding her horse at Saddle Ridge Ranch.

Since her pregnancy, Kylie hadn't been able to take on training horses...or even giving lessons. After her baby was born, she was hoping to jump in again with both feet. Until she could, boarding horses would help keep Saddle Ridge from sinking deeper into debt.

At seven-and-a-half-months pregnant, she was driving herself hard, concentrating on the life growing inside of her, managing Saddle Ridge as well as working as office manager at Wild Horse's temporary employment agency. No wonder she hadn't gotten her hair trimmed in months or applied more than lipstick before she left the ranch every morning.

As she followed the brunette in the short black skirt down the hall to the saloon's office, the hairs on the nape of Kylie's neck prickled. Something about Trish Hammond's demeanor seemed...off. Kylie's hand protectively went to her tummy. The fingers of her other hand gripped her purse tighter.

This is about boarding a horse, she scolded herself. *Relax.*

Yet once she stood inside the small cluttered office and Trish Hammond closed the door, her uneasiness grew. Squaring her shoulders and lifting her chin, she looked the waitress in the eye. "You have one horse to board?"

Trish's red blouse clung to her breasts as she gave an offhanded shrug. "I never *exactly* told you I had a horse to board. I just said I wanted to talk about it. Really, I had another reason for asking you here. I have something you might want. It belonged to your husband."

Trish opened her cowhide purse, the same shade of red as her boots, and extracted something shiny.

Kylie felt suddenly queasy as she recognized the belt buckle. Alex had several of them that he'd won at rodeos. Bull riding had always been his passion...and it had killed him.

Her mouth went dry. Her heart raced. Her worst fears, which had gnawed at her over the past couple of years, had also urged her to hide her head in the sand. Yet she knew she had to play this out. She knew she had to finally face the truth.

Taking the buckle from Trish, she turned it over and saw the engraving on the back. Alex had been dead for four months, but he still had the power to hurt her. The date on the belt buckle was April, the month before she'd gotten pregnant.

When she lifted her gaze to Trish's, she knew this was the woman who'd been calling the ranch and hanging up whenever Alex wasn't home. This was the woman who had been her competitor and she hadn't even known it. It had been Trish's initial on the note on the cocktail napkin Kylie had found when she'd sorted through Alex's clothes.

Why had Trish called her here? To humiliate her? To see for herself the woman Alex had married, yet betrayed? Kylie *could* attack. She could sling accusations. She could show how much she was shaken by this proof that Alex had cared for someone else, maybe as much as he'd cared for her, perhaps even more. But she knew anything she did or said could affect her baby. She could gain satisfaction for a minute, but anxiety from words flung in pain would last a lot longer. Her hands trembled and she wouldn't let Trish Hammond see that.

Whatever Trish's reasons for needing this confrontation, Kylie wouldn't give her the satisfaction of a scene. She laid the buckle on the desk. "If Alex gave that to you, then he wanted you to have it." She turned to leave.

Obviously Trish had wanted to get a much bigger rise out of her because she asked, "Didn't you mind sharing your husband?"

Fury rocked Kylie. She didn't think she'd ever been this angry in her whole life. But she also knew her life with her son or daughter was more important than any hurt this woman could inflict.

Still, she couldn't keep the fierceness from her voice. "I believed in the vows I made. I tried to hold my marriage together, but I couldn't do it alone."

As tears burned her eyes, she turned her back on the other woman and left Clementine's quickly. Outside she blindly made her way to her small blue pickup at the edge of the parking lot. Rooting for her keys, she finally found them as she tried not to think...tried not to feel...tried not to remember.

However, as she climbed into her truck and turned the ignition switch, she *did* remember—the weeks at a time Alex had gone on the road following the circuit, the nights of loneliness, the days of chores and finally facing the fact that Saddle Ridge was sinking deeper and deeper into debt and her husband wouldn't listen to her about it.

Backing out of her parking space, she veered toward the lot's entrance and Wild Horse Way. Once on the road she turned on the heater, knowing she was too cold inside for the warmer air to do any good. Tears began falling then as she relived her decision to leave Alex if he didn't go to a counselor with her. Before he'd left for his last rodeo in Las Vegas, they'd argued. He'd accused her of getting pregnant on purpose to keep him at home more. She'd insisted their marriage didn't stand a chance unless they tried couples' therapy. That had been the main reason for her wanting to take the job at the temp agency. Not only to earn more money to pay for the bills, but to pay for counseling so they could put their marriage back together and maybe start over.

As she avoided a pothole in the road, tears fell harder. She increased her speed outside of town. Her heart hurt so badly she knew it might finally break. Picturing the satisfaction in Trish Hammond's eyes as she'd handed Kylie the belt buckle, Kylie couldn't hold in the sobs that broke loose now.

Distracted, she barely registered the upcoming pothole. As she hit it, her truck listed and fell to the right, banging onto the road. She lost control and, in horror, knew she was going to land in the ravine.

One prayer passed her lips. "Lord, keep my baby safe."

Then the truck lurched sideways and fell sharply, throwing her against the door. When her head hit the steering wheel, a gray fog swept over her. Closing her eyes, she let it engulf her, relieved to escape the pain of a broken heart.

Chapter One

Panic gripped Kylie as Brock Warner entered her room Sunday afternoon. Unfortunately, her enforced stay in the hospital since Friday had given her too much time to remember her confrontation with Trish Hammond. All she'd been able to think about was her husband's infidelity.

Now here was his half brother! How had he found out about her accident? Was he going to try to convince her to sell Saddle Ridge?

"What are you doing here?" Her emotions were so raw the question had just popped out.

Shoving his black Stetson higher on his forehead, Brock stopped beside the chair where Kylie sat. "Dix called me. He was worried sick about you."

Her foreman shouldn't have meddled. "I'm fine."

"Don't you just *look* fine." Brock's thick black eyebrows

quirked up as he took notice of her sling, then the bruise on her forehead.

Her brother-in-law's Apache blood was evident in the hue of his skin, the dark somberness of his eyes and the jet blackness of his hair. Brock Warner emanated a sensuality when he walked, when he talked and when he smiled, in a way she'd seen in few men. It had given her a jumbled, off-balance sensation when she was a teenager…and still did now. She remembered the night she graduated from high school, the night she'd kissed him and—

She stood, pride and courage taking over for her and her unborn child. "I'm sorry Dix dragged you here from… wherever you were."

"Texas," Brock filled in. "Between consultations."

"When did you arrive?" she asked warily, her gaze taking in everything about him. She hadn't seen him since Jack Warner's funeral five years ago…when Brock's new wife had accompanied him.

"I got in about an hour ago. Dix looked worn out, so I offered to come get you."

Concern for Dix took away her annoyance at his interference. He'd been a friend of her father's and had looked out for her in a quiet way since he'd gotten her a job at Saddle Ridge. They were both worn out. Trying to keep the ranch afloat without any outside help had been wearing on them long before Alex had died.

Brock's gaze softened a bit as it slid from her loose blond hair to her maternity top. "I'm sorry about what happened to Alex."

Brock had said that on the phone after he'd missed Alex's funeral. He'd been doing whatever geologists did somewhere in Central America. Away from civilization, he hadn't called his home in Texas for messages in over a week. When he finally had, he'd phoned her and learned about the bull-riding accident that had taken his brother's life. By that time, though, Alex was buried and she hadn't wanted Brock to learn the condition of Saddle Ridge. It was during that phone call she'd told him she was pregnant but managing perfectly fine.

"I'm sorry for your loss, too," she said quietly, knowing Brock had cared deeply about Alex.

"The last time I talked to him he was in Utah. I should have kept in touch more often," Brock said with real regret.

The crack in Kylie's heart grew a little wider when she thought about the last time *she* had talked to Alex. After he'd left early for his last rodeo, she was sure their marriage had been over. With what she'd found out from Trish Hammond, it had been over long before that day.

A smiling nurse bustled into the room, cast an admiring look at Brock, then handed Kylie a few papers. "Here are Dr. Marco's instructions. I understand he went over them with you this morning."

Kylie studied the checklist. For the most part, she was supposed to rest for the next two weeks.

Brock took them from her hands. "I spoke with your doctor a few minutes ago. I told him I'd make sure you followed his recommendations."

"What do you mean *you'll* make sure? Go back to Texas, I don't need you here. Dix should never have called you."

"*You* should have called me long before this. One look at the place—" He shook his head. "There will be time enough for this discussion. Right now, let's get you home."

When Brock took her elbow, Kylie's knees felt wobbly. She could smell the piney musk of his aftershave, feel the strength in his large hand. She had once dreamed of more than friendship with Brock Warner, but he'd dismissed her as too young for his consideration. He'd come home with a wife and that had told Kylie, more than anything else, that she'd never belong in his life.

Six months after that, she'd married Alex.

She and Alex had gone to school together. He'd teased her in the play yard. They'd shared homework. When her pop died and she'd had to sell their homestead to pay debts, when she'd moved to Saddle Ridge and taken a room above the barn to be a groom to the horses, Alex had still seemed more like a brother than a suitor. Then suddenly, after his dad died, he'd turned the full extent of his cowboy charm on her. Not only that, he'd needed her. He'd poured out his grief to her and she'd shared his loss…because she'd lost her own dad. Never one to sit still long enough to figure out numbers, Alex had asked her to help him with the bookkeeping, and he'd found her suggestions made sense. Yet he'd had his own agenda. Marrying her had only been a part of it.

Now, she didn't know if he'd ever really loved her. She had loved him, in a loyal, until-death-do-us-part kind of way. She'd wanted to have children with him. She'd wanted to raise a brood—sons and daughters who would always have each other and the legacy of Saddle Ridge to depend upon. But Alex had wanted to postpone having kids and it wasn't until they'd been married a couple of years that she'd really understood he'd never grown up himself, that he'd intended to ride the rodeo circuit until he was too old to care about conquering the next ornery bull.

When a volunteer came into the room with a wheelchair, Kylie pulled away from Brock's clasp. "I can walk. I don't need—"

"Hospital policy," the nurse announced cheerily.

Brock hefted up the worn, leather duffel bag that had been her pop's. "I'll take this to the car and meet you at the front entrance."

As Brock left the hospital room, Kylie almost felt dizzy with relief. Then she reminded herself the woozy feeling probably had come from the concussion. Concussion or not, she was clearheaded about one important fact—she would *never* depend on Brock Warner. He was not going to look after her…or interfere in her life.

A short time later, Brock picked her up at the hospital's entrance in a white SUV. They'd driven in silence for about five minutes when Kylie cut the awkward tension. "Did you rent this?"

"Yes. For now. But after what happened to your truck, I'll be going to look for something to replace it."

"Dix said it could be repaired."

"It had a broken ball joint and it's fifteen years old. With over one hundred and fifty thousand miles, it's time to let go of it, Kylie."

Holding on to the first vehicle she'd ever owned hadn't been strictly sentimentality. She simply couldn't afford to replace it. "I'll check the paper for used trucks."

"Don't worry about that. I'll take care of it. The ranch could use a new one. What happened to the crew-cab Alex won?"

So Brock had known about that, Kylie realized. Two years ago, a prize at one of the rodeo competitions had been a brand-spanking-new silver truck but it had been a gas guzzler. "I sold it."

"Why didn't you keep it and get rid of yours?"

Because she couldn't have gotten anything for hers. "I did what I thought was best."

The message she sent was clear—the truck she drove was none of his business.

Brock's jaw tightened and deep furrows dented his forehead.

Turning away from him, she stared out the side window. If he thought he could come in here and just ride rough-shod over her, he was sadly mistaken.

"Why didn't you call me and tell me Saddle Ridge was going to hell?" Brock demanded of Dix an hour later.

The pre-Thanksgiving wind held an icy bite as Brock turned from the foreman to scrutinize the outside of the barn, with its peeling paint, the few horses loose in the corral and the acres of land that used to be peppered with at least five hundred head of Angus, but now only boasted about fifty.

Brock shook his head with disbelief.

"Maybe instead of waiting for a call from me, you should have come home to see what was going on."

Brock stared out over the sections of Warner land. "There was no place for me here. There never was, and you know that."

"What I know is that you can be as stubborn as your father was."

His father.

Jack Warner hadn't been a real parent to him, though

he'd fathered him and given him his name. He'd married Brock's mother to save face. The smart, handsome, rich Jack Warner couldn't handle the reputation of being a scoundrel, of sleeping with a woman and then turning his back on her when she got pregnant…even if she *were* Apache. He'd married her and Brock had been born here, but had never felt as if Jack Warner had cared one bit for him. And he'd always known why. His skin was the wrong color. His hair was coal-black, like his mother's, not blond like his father's. The bottom line was Jack had never loved Brock's mother. He hadn't really wanted her as a wife. He'd never wanted Brock.

Brock glanced over at the house where he'd grown up but never really belonged. The roof was missing a few shingles and the porch steps looked as if they should be replaced. "When did this start happening?"

"After your daddy passed."

That brought Brock's gaze to Dix's again. "Alex let it go like this?"

"You think this happened in the four months since he died? Look again, son. This neglect has taken years. Kylie's worked harder than any man I know. The two of us have tried to keep up, but we couldn't. With Alex gone so much—"

"Bull riding?"

"Bull riding. Chasing the next belt buckle or purse. Always expecting to win the Grand Championship and never doin' it. I do understand why you didn't come back here since your daddy died. His will was a slap in the face, leaving the place to Alex, and only giving you half of it if he sold it. But why didn't you come back here after *Alex* died?"

"I was in a jungle. I never got the message about Alex until after the funeral. I called Kylie then. Didn't she tell you?"

"No, she didn't. What did she tell *you?*"

"She mentioned she was pregnant, but she said everything was fine."

"And just what else was she supposed to say with you in another country and her here?"

"She could have told me the truth."

"In Kylie's mind, she probably *was* fine," Dix admitted, blowing out a huge breath. "She has plans to turn this place around after the baby's born."

"What kind of plans?"

"Teaching more classes. Boarding more horses. Training more two-year-olds."

"She's dreaming."

"Yes, she is. About her baby's future. She didn't tell you what was going on because she didn't want you to know, is my guess. You proved you didn't care about Saddle Ridge by staying away. I wouldn't have called you, except the doc says she's supposed to take it easy for the next couple of weeks. I knew I couldn't handle this myself. I hate admitting it, but it's true." Dix's red beard was laced with some gray now. The lines on his weathered face were deep and counted every one of his sixty-two years.

"No hands at all? Not even part-time?"

"We couldn't afford them! I shouldn't even be talking to you about this. Kylie should. But she's still shaken up and I don't want her worrying so much. It's not good for her or the baby."

Brock had been back home in Texas when Dix had

called him yesterday to tell him about Kylie's accident. He didn't know what to make of any of this.

After his dad had divorced his mom, she'd gone back to live with her family on a reservation in Arizona. He'd been four years old, and he could still remember the tears in her eyes when she'd claimed Saddle Ridge was where his future lay. As he'd grown older, he'd understood what she'd meant. If he stayed at the ranch, he could eventually go to college and become anything he wanted to be. If he went to Arizona and lived on the reservation with her, he wouldn't be happy. He wouldn't get the same kind of education. He wouldn't grow up to be everything a man could be.

He'd visited his mother, mostly in the summers, but his life had been empty without her. Jack Warner had never been warm to Brock. He'd hired a housekeeper, and Brock had had all his needs met. But after Jack remarried and Alex was born, with his blond hair and his blue eyes just like his mom and dad, Brock often thought about leaving and going to live with his mother in Arizona. Yet as each year passed and his mother encouraged him to stay, he'd bonded with his half brother, found satisfaction in school work and tending to the horses, and he'd always felt a kinship with the land.

"With the holidays comin'," Dix continued, "Kylie's driving herself harder. She's on a committee for the First Night celebration in town. She has presents to make, as well as things to ready for the baby."

"The last thing she needs to be worried about is Christmas presents, decorations and a New Year's Eve party."

"Don't go tellin' her that, or you'll get your head handed

to you on a platter. You might anyway," he muttered. "She likes to do everything on her own."

"Didn't you call me so I'd get back here and talk some sense into her?"

"Not exactly. I called you because she needs help. *I* need help. You've got a vested interest in this place—"

"The terms of the will apply to Kylie the same as they did to Alex. I've only got a vested interest if she sells it." Brock zipped up his windbreaker. He'd have to get warmer clothes if he was going to stay here through the winter.

Through the winter. When had he made *that* decision?

"You *are* going to help, aren't you?" Dix asked now, looking worried, maybe wondering if the boy he'd known had become a man who was different from that boy.

"Yes, I'll help. I have paperwork to finish on a project and a few loose ends to tie up, but nothing else is pending right now."

"It won't be a hardship to take some time off?"

Brock knew Dix meant financially. He made more money than he knew what to do with. Maybe because he worked all the time, more often than not in locations where most men wouldn't go. Maybe because saving had always been more important than immediate gratification. He'd also invested in a few wells over the years that had hit big. A few months on Saddle Ridge wouldn't be a problem. A few months until Kylie's baby was born…until Alex's baby was born.

"No hardship."

"Kylie's had a lot on her shoulders, son. Remember that," Dix warned him.

He'd remember that. Unfortunately, staying at Saddle

Ridge he'd remember a lot more. He'd have to face the fact those memories still might have power over him.

While he was here this time, he'd shake loose of their power for good.

An hour later Brock stepped over the threshold once more into the two-story ranch house. Immediately he spotted Kylie on the sofa, stretched out, asleep. She looked like a pregnant princess. But he knew she'd never been coddled like a princess. He knew she'd always been a hard worker, intent on living each day to its fullest.

Now what? His brother's wife was smack-dab in the middle of a ranch that needed manpower, capital and something much more intangible to invigorate it. Why hadn't Alex done something about the condition of the place? Why hadn't he asked for help if he'd needed it? Because of pride? Whether he and Alex had wanted to admit it or not, Jack Warner had fostered competition between them. There was nothing to compete over. As a child, Brock had known he'd never have his father's affection.

This place brought back memories Brock didn't want to revisit, and he focused on the physical surroundings. Some of the furniture was newer than the rest. Dix had informed him that new furniture had been Alex's wedding present to Kylie.

Some wedding present, Brock thought. It was striped teal-and-wine with huge, rolled arms and Brock suspected Kylie had chosen it rather than Alex having picked it out as a surprise. Automatically, Brock thought about the strand of Tahitian pearls he'd given Marta before *their* wedding. She'd loved them. She'd said she loved him. But she couldn't have walked away so easily if she had. He couldn't have gotten over her so quickly if *he* had loved her the way a husband should love a wife.

Love. Lust. Convenience. Need. Physical satisfaction. Who knew how much any of that played into a relationship? Who really knew how to figure out what was love and what was something else?

Watching Kylie like this, he was transported back to a night in the barn when she'd been seventeen and he'd been twenty-two, home for her graduation…and Alex's. Proud of her, he'd given her a present. She'd kissed him. For a few moments he'd forgotten she was underage and he was a hell of a lot more experienced. But after those few moments, he'd ended it, backed away and done what was best for both of them. Later that weekend, Alex had informed him he was going to marry Kylie someday.

Brock had returned to his Ph.D. work, focused on life away from Saddle Ridge and married Marta shortly after he'd met her. Too soon, too fast, too different.

As if Kylie could feel his gaze on her, she opened her blue eyes, then pushed herself into a sitting position. Her hair fell over her shoulders as she did, and Brock remembered tugging her ponytail to tease her. He remembered how the night she'd kissed him, he'd threaded his fingers into the silky strands.

"I thought you might be hungry," he said gruffly. "How do you feel? And don't tell me fine."

"My shoulder's hurting," she admitted, adjusting the sling.

As she began to rise, he moved toward the sofa. "What do you need?"

Her eyes were troubled when they met his. "An ice pack."

"The doc gave you something for pain, didn't he?"

"I won't put medication in my body if I don't have to…because of the baby."

"Stay put," he ordered. "I'll get the ice."

Returning to her with the pack wrapped in a towel, he asked, "Do you want to take the sling off?"

"I guess I have to."

Before he reconsidered what he was doing, he sat next to her and helped her remove the sling. As she lifted her hair and he slipped the sling over her head, his palm brushed the side of her cheek. His pulse raced, and he decided it was an adrenaline shot because he didn't want to hurt her. However, when the sling lay in her lap and he pressed the ice pack to her shoulder, the adrenaline didn't stop and his heart pounded hard against his chest.

Her cornflower-blue eyes shimmered a bit before she closed them.

"Kylie?"

"I'm fine," she murmured, not opening her eyes.

"Those are two words you're not going to use around me. Remember?" Ever since he'd known her, she'd never let anyone know she *wasn't* fine.

"When did you become such a bully?" she grumbled.

"When I moved to Texas, I found life on my own and getting my own way was a heck of a lot more fun than trying to please anyone here."

Her eyes opened then and a bit of the shimmer remained. "You always get your own way in Texas?"

He chuckled. "Most of the time." Then when he considered his life there, he became serious. "There are people in Texas who respect me." His friends and colleagues didn't care that he had Apache blood…and didn't look at him as if he were an outsider.

"There are people *here* who respect you."

"I needed to be away from Saddle Ridge to find my life."

"Have you found it?"

"Yes," he answered tersely, then changed the subject. "Are you hungry?"

"No. But I have to eat for the baby."

Although he'd been trying to ignore her rounded tummy, now his gaze dropped to it. "Do you know if it's a boy or a girl?"

"I want to be surprised."

"What did Alex want?" he asked, curious.

"I'm sure he wanted a boy. Don't all men?"

He could tell she was trying too hard to give him a smile. What was going on behind those eyes? "Maybe. Maybe not."

Their gazes met again and he felt too much. This time he broke eye contact and glanced around the room. Suddenly he realized what was missing. "Where's your TV?"

"I don't have time to watch TV."

"That's not what I asked you. At Christmas last year, Alex said he bought himself a big-screen plasma TV so he could watch his tapes and improve his rodeo technique."

Taking the ice pack and moving it to a different part of her shoulder, she asked, "Does it matter?"

"It might. What happened to it?"

"I needed the money from it to pay bills."

Brock didn't like the picture that was coming into clearer focus. "I want to look at the books."

Again her expression was troubled. "I can't prevent you from doing that."

"But you'd like to. Why?"

Her cheeks became rosy with color. "On your own admission, you couldn't wait to leave here. You rarely came back after you went to school. You haven't come back since your dad died. So why do you want to get involved now?"

The problem was, he couldn't give her just one reason. The problem was, he wasn't certain why he was here or what he expected from coming home. It wasn't his place now, though—it was hers. Unless she decided to sell it. "I came back because Dix admitted he couldn't handle you and the ranch."

"I'm going to be—" She stopped.

"It'll be at least two weeks—maybe longer—until you're really back on your feet. That's what the doctor said. By then you'll be dealing with the last two months of your pregnancy. How much do you think you'll be able to help Dix? Face reality, Kylie."

Without any warning she let the ice pack drop to the sofa and stood. "I've faced more reality than you can ever imagine. So don't preach to me, Brock." She headed out of the living room to a hall at the back of the house.

"Where are you going?" he demanded.

"To the bathroom. Don't think you're going to follow me there."

Brock raked his hand through his hair. Making Kylie's supper would be the easy part. Sitting together and pretending there weren't issues and problems to be resolved between them would be the difficult part. With her pregnancy and all, she really should be staying on the first floor. After Jack had had a heart attack a few years before he died, he'd renovated the downstairs, closing the back porch into a bedroom and modernizing and expanding the bath so it included a shower. Kylie should really be spending the latter part of her pregnancy down here. He could help her move her things. But right now wasn't the time to suggest it. Maybe after he'd cooked them a meal, maybe after they'd talked superficially about something other than Saddle Ridge, she'd relax around him and he'd relax around her.

A little devil in his ear told him he was dreaming if he thought *that* was going to happen.

The bottom line here was he had to tread carefully. He had to remind himself she was still grieving over Alex, and the loss would be with her for a long time. If he tried to take over, he might trample everything she held dear. Then she'd hate him.

He couldn't abide the thought of Kylie Armstrong Warner hating him. That realization made him decidedly uneasy.

Leaning back in his kitchen chair, Brock swiped at his mouth with his napkin and tossed it onto thc table. His plate was clean. Frustration with Kylie was growing minute by minute. Frustration with himself for caring how she was reacting to him wasn't much better. The fact that his gut twisted every time she smiled had him totally unsettled. He was damned uncomfortable.

"When are you going to stop pretending with me?" he asked, hoping to clear the air. For the past fifteen minutes she'd pushed food around on her plate, not eating much of anything. He suspected she was hurting but she wouldn't admit it.

"We've known each other for years," he went on. "I won't be insulted if you don't like the way I cooked the steak."

She studied him for a moment. "We spent some time together years ago on your short visits home. I haven't laid eyes on you for five years. I'm not sure we *do* know each other."

Okay, he'd asked for that. Maybe he should have put things a different way. "Years ago, you said what you were thinking. You were as easy to read as the proverbial open book. Now you're acting as if you want me to go away and never come back when it's obvious you need help here. I'm trying to make sense of what's going on. Alex never mentioned this place was headed downstream. Why not?"

Her answer was quick coming. "Do you *really* think he'd tell you? He'd *never* want you to know that he'd failed to succeed in managing what Jack had left him."

"What if I'd come back and seen it?"

"But you didn't. The decline of Saddle Ridge didn't happen overnight. It's been slow. There were times when I thought that with or without Alex's help I could turn it around—"

She stopped.

"What do you mean with or *without* Alex's help?"

The guarded expression was back on her face, the shadows in her eyes.

"Why wouldn't Alex want to keep Saddle Ridge going?" he pressed.

"Oh, he wanted to keep it going. Rather, he wanted *me* to keep it going."

"And what was *he* doing?" Brock asked cautiously.

"You know what he was doing. He was riding the rodeo circuit, chasing the wildest bull."

That's what Dix had said. Brock thought about the times Alex had called him. Often he'd been away from Saddle Ridge. And whenever Brock had called Alex—those times had been too few—at Alex's direction, he'd gotten hold of him on his cell phone.

So Kylie wouldn't answer?

The same tension that had looped around them ever since he'd stepped into Kylie's hospital room surrounded them now. It was broken when the door opened and Dix came in.

The foreman took off his Stetson and when he entered the kitchen, he looked like a man who was facing his executioner. "Are you still talking to me?" he asked Kylie.

"Do I have any choice?" she returned with a half smile that told Brock she couldn't stay mad at Dix for long.

"You do," the older man answered, "but the horses don't like a woman in a snit any more than I do."

She laughed. The sound was so genuine, so free, that Brock remembered the girl she'd been.

"Well then, that decides it," she said, getting to her feet and wincing because she'd moved too fast.

Every protective instinct in Brock urged him to push back his chair, put his arm around her shoulders and make sure she got to the sofa safely. Yet he stayed put because he knew she wouldn't tolerate it.

Kylie was lifting her plate to take it to the sink when Brock said, "I'll get the dishes."

Dix's gaze cut from one of them to the other. "Looks like everything's under control in here," he muttered.

"In a week I'll be back in the barn," Kylie told him.

"Only to visit." Brock's voice was steel.

"You don't have anything to worry about," Dix assured her. "Feather's doing fine. She even let me put a blanket on her rump this afternoon. Of course she does miss you, but I'll tend to her real good."

"Feather?" Brock asked.

"I adopted a mustang from the B.L.M."

The Bureau of Land Management thinned the wild mustang herds that roamed the western rangelands, then they put the horses up for adoption. The mustangs were descendants of the Spanish horses and, when trained, made great riding mounts with stout constitutions. But not just anyone had the patience to gentle a wild mustang. Kylie obviously did.

Reflexively, his gaze went to her rounding tummy. She'd make a wonderful mother. He'd seen her patience and kindness as she'd interacted with horses. She'd be the same with children.

"Thanks, Dix. I don't know what I'd do without you." The sincerity in her voice said she meant every word.

Flushing, her foreman dropped his hat back on his head. "I'll be in my quarters if you need me."

This afternoon Brock had learned Dix resided in the old apartment over the barn where Kylie had stayed when she'd moved to the ranch. The bunkhouse, which once housed four to six hands, no longer had running water or electricity. Brock still didn't understand what had happened here, and he intended to find out.

Every step Kylie took to the sofa seemed to be an effort, and Brock knew she was hurting. She was so petite, her pregnancy mainly showed at her tummy. Her cheeks might be a tiny bit fuller, her breasts might be a little bigger—

He stopped that thought before it could form. He stopped that thought before a picture went with it. She was a pregnant woman, for God's sake! He couldn't be attracted to her.

Could he? Hadn't he always noticed Kylie, but—being five years older—kept away from her? After Alex had declared his intentions to marry her and kept declaring them until he did it, Brock had stepped away for good. She was still his brother's wife. She was still carrying his brother's baby. And she loved Saddle Ridge.

He'd almost hated it. He'd hated what Jack Warner had felt about it. He'd hated the fact that his father had left it to his brother. He'd hated all the memories that had made him feel like a second-class citizen and his mother an outcast. Everyone had known Jack hadn't loved Conchita Vasco. He'd done his duty by her. When he'd met someone else who was his kind, who would produce the blond son he'd craved, he'd divorced Brock's mother and never cared about seeing her again. He'd been a cold man. When his new wife had been diagnosed with breast cancer and died a few years later, he'd turned even colder.

Coming back here had rubbed every one of Brock's nerves raw. Being around Kylie wasn't helping. The best solution for both of them was to sell Saddle Ridge and move on. But he had the feeling that wasn't anywhere in her plans.

Brock was dropping plates into the dishwasher when the phone rang. Out of the corner of his eye, he saw Kylie reach for the cordless on the end table by the sofa. She obviously knew the person on the other end because she propped a pillow at the sofa's arm and curled into it, trying to make herself comfortable.

In spite of himself, Brock wondered about her life now. What had she done in her free time before she'd become pregnant? Did she still ride into the Painted Peaks, hoping to glimpse the bands of mustangs that hadn't inhabited the mountains for years? Did she ever return to Devil's Canyon in the Bighorns and feel as if she were standing on top of the world? He'd taken her there once…the day before her graduation.

Why was he remembering that now? Why was he remembering the peace and awe on her face as she'd studied the striated cliffs, the gorge, the river below? Why could he still remember her absolute delight when she'd spotted a band of mustangs?

He'd learned "why" wasn't a good question to ask. *What should he do?* was more easily answered. Action won over philosophizing any day.

Fifteen minutes later, the kitchen cleaned up, a pot of coffee brewed and a mug in his hand, he no longer heard Kylie's voice on the phone.

Going to the living room he sat in the armchair across from her. "A friend calling to see if you got home safe and sound?"

The smile left her face, and at first he thought she was going to put those guards up again. Instead, she asked, "Do you remember Shaye Bartholomew?"

He remembered both girls Kylie had run with. Shaye was a brunette and Gwen Langworthy had auburn curls that had bobbed everywhere. "I remember Shaye. Her father was a doctor—a cardiologist."

"Yes. He still is. At least until the New Year. Then, from what Shaye says, he's going to retire."

"I'm surprised Shaye stayed in Wild Horse Junction. She was a smart girl."

"Smart girls leave?" Kylie asked with a hint of amusement.

"If I remember correctly, Shaye was headed off to college." Kylie had been smart, too, so smart she'd skipped a grade and was a year younger than her friends. But she'd never had aspirations to go to college or to leave Wild Horse Junction. Not as far as Brock knew.

"Right now she's a social worker part-time. Last February, Dylan Malloy's sister died. He was probably a year or two ahead of you in school. Anyway, his sister had a baby right before she passed on, and her will made Shaye legal guardian."

"Not her brother?"

"After Dylan's and Julia's parents died, he'd given up his own dreams to get his sister out of foster care. She lived with him. I guess as an adult, she hadn't wanted to burden him again with a baby. But along the way of figuring out whether Shaye or Dylan would be the best parent for Julia's son, they fell in love. They just married in July."

"What about Gwen? Are you still in touch with her?"

"Sure am. She's an obstetrical nurse practitioner. She's getting married after Christmas and I'm her matron of honor."

Bypassing details of the wedding, he remarked, "You said you're due the end of January. When's your exact due date?" He was surprised she was going to be in a wedding that late in her pregnancy.

"January twenty-ninth. I'll be as big as a house, but Gwen didn't seem to care. Both Shaye and I are standing up for her."

"I'm surprised the three of you are still close. That doesn't often happen—childhood friends holding on until adulthood."

"No, I guess it doesn't. But we were always more like sisters than friends. Shaye asked me to come for Thanksgiving dinner, but her place will be bedlam with all her family. I'm not sure I'll be ready for that by Thursday."

"Wise choice."

"I'm glad you approve," she responded somewhat acerbically.

"Kylie, I didn't mean to make it sound—"

"As if you know best?" she interrupted. "That's exactly how you've made it sound ever since you arrived." Shifting to the edge of the sofa, she used her good arm to push herself up. "I think I'm going to turn in. It's early, but the doctor said to rest, so that's what I'm going to do."

She knew he wasn't about to refute the doctor's orders. She could make her escape and he'd be left with his thoughts, as well as the mess Saddle Ridge was in.

"Where's your computer?" he asked.

"In the spare room upstairs. Why?"

"Because I want to start going over the books."

"Tonight? I really should show you the program I use."

"I'm computer savvy. I have to be with the work I do. I can figure out almost any program. Do you have a problem with me looking at the records?"

"Would it matter if I did?" she asked with a sigh.

"No, not if you want me to help you."

"That's the problem, Brock. I don't know if I want your help, not only for my sake, but for yours. You don't want to be here. You don't want to be involved with Saddle Ridge."

"You're my sister-in-law. Family helps family."

"Like Jack and Alex helped you?"

"I didn't need Alex's help. And Jack? Well, he put me through college. That's one of the reasons my mother left me here with him. He gave me my future, so I really can't complain."

"He never gave you the love and care you needed. You have every right to complain," she said softly…compassionately.

"Let's not get into that, Kylie. The past is what it was. Now Jack and Alex are gone, and you have decisions to make."

"Such as?"

"Such as whether or not you're going to sell Saddle Ridge and start a really good life with the proceeds."

She frowned. "Which you'll get half of."

He studied her for a few seconds. "You think that's why I came?"

"I'm still not sure why you came."

Since he wasn't, either, he was going to let that subject drop. But then he said, "I didn't come here to hurt you. I know you're grieving. I know you miss Alex and the life you had. I also know it's better not to make major decisions right after a loved one dies. But you really have no choice."

"I'm managing," she protested.

"That's why I want to look at the books. To see if you are."

She put a weary hand to her forehead.

He thought it trembled a little. "We'll talk about this tomorrow. In the meantime, don't you think you should be sleeping downstairs?"

"Why?"

"It would be safer. If you need things from up there, I can bring them down."

The expression on her face brought him to his feet because he knew she was going to fight him on this and probably everything else.

"You were Alex's older brother, Brock, not mine. You say you want to help. Fine. There's not much I can do about that. But helping doesn't mean changing the way I live my life. Helping means taking some of the burden off of Dix. Helping means getting to know Feather until I can get back out into the barn. Helping means looking at my agenda, not setting one of your own. If you can help in those ways, I'd be more than grateful if you'd stay. But if you came here with the idea that I'm going to put Saddle Ridge up for sale and sell it to a developer so you can wipe away the memories and pretend you weren't raised here, it's *not* going to happen."

Her blue eyes were shiny with emotion now. "I love this ranch. Every hill and valley, every fence post, every floorboard that creaks. It's my son or daughter's future. A way of life that's vanishing. I won't let it vanish for him or her." She went to the stairway and took hold of the banister. "I'll be careful, Brock. Believe me, I will." She started up the steps.

Her shoulders held a courageous line, and in spite of the friction between them, he wanted to take her into his arms and tell her everything was going to be all right. But that was the last thing he intended to do. Truthfully, he didn't know if everything *would* be all right. How could it be, when her husband was dead and she was in debt up to her pretty little ears? He had to find out how much. He had to find out what it would take to dig her out.

"As soon as I warm up my coffee, I'll work up in the spare room."

She stopped and looked over her shoulder. "Do whatever you need to do. I'll see you in the morning."

He watched her until she reached the top of the stairs. Then she disappeared into the hall shadows. Moments later, he heard her bedroom door close.

Those had been tears in her eyes as she'd defended her dreams, and he felt like a heel for causing them. Snatching up his mug, he took it to the kitchen, hearing his father's voice echo sarcastically in his head. *Welcome home, Brock.*

He refilled his mug, determined to block out his father's indifference, along with the turmoil returning here had caused.

Chapter Two

When Kylie awakened, her room was pitch-black. No moon gave even an inkling of light. It was this time of night when she missed Alex most, and she wasn't even sure why. What she missed was the way they'd been together after they first married. What she missed was the friendship and true caring they'd once shared. Over the past year, Alex had been away more than he'd been home. In the middle of the night, she'd often awakened, wishing he were there holding her, smiling at her in that crooked, boyish way he had. The daytime hours were so busy and passed so fast, she didn't have time to think. At night she did. She had time to think, feel and miss what might have been.

She had turned in early because she'd been hurting and because she'd had to escape Brock's questions as well as the look of censure in his eyes. The corner of her heart that at seventeen had thought he could do no wrong begged to be unlocked. But if she unlocked it, all of her fears and worries and regrets would come pouring out. She didn't know if it was safe to give any of those to Brock. Her encounter with Trish Hammond was a sore that wouldn't heal. She badly needed salve for it. When she had some time alone with Gwen and Shaye, she'd probably tell them about it. But it wasn't something she could discuss easily. It wasn't anything she could discuss when other people were around. It was embarrassing and humiliating and so deep-down painful, sometimes it took her breath away.

Alex had been unfaithful.

For how long? With more women than Trish? At the moment, she felt like Brock, wanting to evade or dismiss the past. She knew, in the long run, whatever happened to her would make her stronger. Still…right now she just plain hurt, emotionally and physically. Tears welled up in her eyes and she let them dribble down her cheeks. But then she stopped the self-pity, and as she had so often over the past months, she thought about her child.

Reaching to the nightstand, her fingers wrapped around her solution to insomnia—her tape player. There was a stack of cassettes there, too. She'd collected them over the years, and now switched on R. Carlos Nakai's Christmas music.

The haunting notes of flutes and bells had her rubbing her tummy tenderly. "What do you think, baby? I know this is one of your favorites. You always settle down when I play this one."

Her baby was a kicker, especially—it seemed—in the middle of the night. But this music always seemed to calm her little one, as well as her. Even if she didn't sleep while it played, she rested. Sweet visions of the mountains and the mustangs and the water rippling calm and serene filled the darkest time of night.

Using a technique she'd learned from a yoga class she'd taken with Gwen and Shaye many years before, she consciously relaxed her muscles, breathing out stress, breathing in peace.

Two soft raps on the door broke her focused concentration. "Kylie? Are you okay?"

"If I say I'm fine, will you throw a fit?"

She didn't hear his sigh or see the roll of his eyes, but she knew he probably did both.

He answered gruffly, "You have a concussion."

Yes, she did. The doctor had told her it would be better if she weren't alone for the next few days. He'd probably told Dix the same thing. That's why Brock was here. Some misguided sense of duty. He'd gotten the full gift of responsibility that Alex had lacked.

She switched off the tape player. "If you want to come in and see for yourself I'm not in a coma, feel free." Propping herself a little higher on the pillows, she turned on the bedside lamp.

The doorknob turned, the door opened and then Brock was standing there in her bedroom, looking as if he'd rather be anywhere else on earth.

"I can tell you my name, where I live and who's President of the United States," she assured him.

"Has anyone ever mentioned that you can be the most frustrating woman on the planet?"

"Not within the last year or so. But I imagine Dix would like to at least once a day."

Finally, Brock's lips twitched up at the corners. "Is the music for you or the baby?"

"That's a toss-up. Sometimes it settles him or her down so I can fall asleep again."

"How's the shoulder?"

"If I don't move, it's not so bad."

"Do you need ice? You didn't bring any up with you."

"Sometimes the ice bag makes me feel like a popsicle. I was going to try to relax into oblivion." He was still wearing his jeans and snap-button shirt. Obviously he hadn't turned in yet. "Have you been on the computer this whole time?"

"Actually, not *your* computer, but mine. I got a call after you went to bed. I'm finishing up a data summary and analysis for a job I did last month. The company's having a board meeting on Monday and the CEO would like it by Friday. I'll get to your books, just not tonight. I'll catch a couple of hours of sleep before I check the cattle with Dix."

"Does that mean you're not going to watch my every move the rest of the day?"

His dark eyes stayed pinned to her. "It means I'll set out everything you need for breakfast and be back in to get you lunch. Don't even try to argue. For the next few days, just consider yourself pampered."

Kylie had never been pampered. The idea that Brock was going to do it made her feel all warm and tingly inside. Maybe she should just give in and enjoy a few days of rest.

All of a sudden the baby started a kicking storm. Her hand went to her tummy and she smiled.

"You felt something?" Brock asked, coming a few steps closer.

"Whether I've got a boy or a girl, he or she will probably be a kick boxer." Something in Brock's expression made her ask, "Do you want to feel?"

In that moment, any camaraderie she'd felt with him fled. Heavy silence intensified the sound of the beating of her heart. She was wearing a flannel nightgown. When she'd shifted higher on her pillows, the coverlet had slipped and was only halfway covering her tummy. Nevertheless, she felt as if Brock could see right through her, could see beneath the quilt and her nightgown to the baby underneath.

"I think I'll pass," he responded, his voice low and deep.

Because he didn't want to touch her? Because he didn't want to touch Alex's child? Because this baby was Jack Warner's heir and could inherit Brock's share of Saddle Ridge if she held onto the ranch? He had to resent her and the baby. There was no way they could have a common goal. No way he could help bring her dreams to fruition without trampling on his.

Had she thought they'd bond over Alex's child? How naive could she get?

She'd been foolish to suggest that he feel her baby kick. She'd made an awkward situation even more awkward, and anything she said now would just make matters worse.

Pulling the covers up to her chin, she looked away from his nearly black eyes, looked away from the beard stubble on his jaw, looked away from the man who had intrigued her almost all of her life.

"Good night, Brock," she almost whispered, tired of always trying to figure out the best thing to do, tired of feeling as if she were always swimming upstream against currents she'd never defeat.

"Good night, Kylie," he returned, then left her room and closed the door.

Her throat tightened and she fought back tears, hating the hormone shifts that accompanied pregnancy. She thought about her wedding day and the album tucked away in the closet. She considered the days and nights Alex had been away and she'd been here alone. Then to her dismay, she all too vividly remembered the kiss she'd given Brock when she was seventeen and the way he'd kissed her back, just for a few moments. She felt guilty thinking about it, as if she were betraying Alex in some way. She'd wanted to be his wife. She'd expected their marriage to work. She'd thought they could be together more than they were apart.

One question played loudly in her head. What would have happened if Brock hadn't come to Jack Warner's funeral with a wife on his arm?

She didn't have the answer to that one and expected she never would.

Kylie descended the steps the following morning, surprised she had slept so late. It was 10:00 a.m., and she never slept past 6:00. But she supposed her body was trying to heal itself. It *was* healing itself and keeping her baby safe.

When she reached the kitchen, she spotted the cereal on the table, the toaster pushed to the edge of the counter and the place set for her. It was as if Brock didn't even want her on tiptoes reaching into the cupboards.

His words when she'd asked if he wanted to feel the baby were still clear in her head. *I think I'll pass.* He was taking care of her out of misguided duty. He didn't really want to be involved.

Suddenly, the front door opened and Brock came inside, along with a rush of cold, Wyoming air. He was wearing a down parka that looked like one of Dix's, and his Stetson was pulled low. "I thought you might be getting up around now. How do you feel?"

"Better," she responded, then assured him, "Really."

Unzipping his coat, he hung it on the hook in the kitchen, then plopped his hat on the hat caddy beside the door. "I'm going to make a pot of coffee. I want to ride the parameters of the property and see just what condition the land is in."

"You remember how to ride?" she teased.

"That's not something I'll ever be likely to forget. Sometimes on a site I've ridden to hard-to-reach places."

"Hard to reach and dangerous?" she asked, thinking about the continents and countries where he might have found oil.

"Sometimes. That's when the pay was really good."

"Did your wife go with you? I know she was a geologist, too."

"Ex-wife," he reminded her, his shoulders more rigid, his deep brown eyes on the alert. "At the beginning, we worked jobs together. Then she got tired of the traveling and decided to take a staff job in Houston."

"You didn't want to take that kind of position?"

"Not particularly. I like the field work."

Suddenly she wanted to know a lot more. "Is that what caused a rift between you?"

The clock ticked, the furnace fan switched on and finally Brock answered, "It doesn't matter what happened between us. It's over."

After a brief hesitation, she asked, "Did you want it to be over? Or did she?"

"It was a mutual decision."

She thought of Alex on the road. A husband and wife couldn't have a marriage if one of them wasn't there.

Although she didn't say the thought aloud, Brock must have read her mind because he added defensively, "There was more than one reason why we divorced."

"Do you still see her?"

"Enough questions, Kylie." He looked angry and she didn't know if that was because she was digging into his past, because she'd touched a nerve or because he was simply a private man.

Going to the coffeepot, he took it from the machine, filled the carafe with water and dumped it into the back.

"I didn't mean to pry," she said softly.

"Yes, you did. But what's happened in my life has nothing to do with what's going on here now."

She wasn't so sure of that. However, she took his very strong hint and changed the subject. "Speaking of what's happening here now, how's Feather?"

"She's a looker," he agreed. "Wary of me."

"She won't be for long if you're patient with her."

"We'll see. Dix said you have a special oatmeal treat you give her."

She pointed to a stoneware canister on the counter. "I make them myself when I have time. There's about half a jar there. She also loves licorice hard candy."

"I'll remember that the next time I get into town. You'd better eat breakfast or it's going to be time for lunch."

As the coffee bubbled and brewed, Kylie went to the refrigerator for the container of milk. It was a gallon jug and more economical to buy it that way. But the container was still three quarters full and heavy.

Brock saw her go for the handle and was quickly beside her, his hand covering hers. "I'll get it."

She didn't argue. She usually used two hands to maneuver it.

At the table he asked, "Do you want a glass of milk besides what's on your cereal?"

"Half a glass."

After he poured the milk into the bowl and the glass, he set the jug on the table and really studied her. They were standing close—close enough that she could smell the pine of his aftershave, the scent of Brock that hadn't changed all these years. She'd pulled the upper part of her hair back in a ponytail and let the rest flow long. Now he touched her forehead beneath her bangs. With anyone else she probably would have shied away. The area where she'd hit her head was tender.

His thumb was calloused, but oh, so gentle as it traced the edges of the bruise. "It's changing color. It'll be gone in a few days."

"I hope my shoulder heals as quickly. There are so many things I want to be doing."

"Like?"

"Like finishing making Christmas gifts. Like decorating for the holidays. Like getting the nursery ready. Like doing anything in the barn I possibly can. I can't stay out of the barn, Brock. I need the smell of hay to live."

Shaking his head, his hand tenderly cupped her cheek. "You can breathe in the hay. You just can't shovel it or move it. When you're feeling better, you can feed Feather her snacks. But that's about it, Kylie. You know it and so do I."

His touch on her skin sent tingling through her body. Why was she reacting like this? Because she already missed being held? Because she missed the intimacy between a man and a woman? Because when Brock touched her, she felt cared for and almost cherished in a way she'd never felt with Alex?

This was wrong…for both of them. When she stepped away from him, his eyes became flat and unreadable.

The front door flew open. Gwen Langworthy and Garrett Maxwell tumbled inside.

Seeing her in the kitchen, Gwen called, "Dix told us to come on in."

Gwen was carrying a chocolate bundt cake wrapped in plastic wrap.

In his arms Garrett lugged a huge carton. Taking it to the kitchen, he set it on the table. "I've got meat loaf and scalloped potatoes, a tray of lasagna and a frozen apple pie."

Kylie's eyes misted. "You shouldn't have gone to all of this trouble."

Maneuvering around the table, Gwen gave Kylie a hug. "No trouble. We had to eat. I just made double."

"Garrett, this is Brock Warner, Alex's brother. Brock, this is Garrett Maxwell, Gwen's fiancé."

Brock shook the man's hand. "Congratulations are in order. You're marrying after Christmas?"

"December twenty-eighth," Garrett answered with a grin.

Brock turned to Gwen. "And I remember you from the days you came riding here after Kylie moved in. You haven't changed."

"I don't know if that's good or bad," Gwen responded wryly. She patted Kylie's shoulder. "We can't stay and visit with you now. We have a meeting with a contractor this afternoon to talk about enlarging Garrett's house."

"So there will be room for Tiffany and the baby?"

"For them or just for us. We want Tiffany and Amy to stay as long as they need to," Garrett interjected. "But already Tiffany is talking about getting an apartment with another young mother in the spring."

"I'm going to miss them terribly when they leave," Gwen admitted.

Kylie briefly filled in Brock. "Someone left a baby inside Gwen's sunroom. After a search, she and Garrett found Tiffany, the young mom who hadn't wanted to give up her baby, but hadn't known what else to do. Gwen took them both in."

"It was a kind thing to do," Brock said.

Garrett dropped his arm around Gwen's shoulders. "She likes mothering. If Tiffany and Amy move out, we'll just have to work on producing some kids of our own."

Her cheeks flushed, Gwen murmured, "Well, they aren't going anywhere yet. And that's another reason we stopped by. How would the two of you like to join us for Thanksgiving dinner? Garrett's mom is flying in and my dad and a lady he's seeing will be joining us, too, along with Tiffany and Amy, of course."

Before Kylie could consider the invitation, Brock broke in. "The doctor wants Kylie to rest. Especially for the first week. She's still pretty sore and tired and—"

"I'm right here, Brock. I can answer for myself." She gazed up at Gwen. "I'd really love to come, but I can't. I have to take care of myself and the baby. Maybe next week we can get together. I should be feeling a lot better by then." She glanced up at Brock. "You could consider going for Thanksgiving dinner at Gwen's."

Appearing startled at that suggestion, he shook his head. "On Wednesday I'm picking up a turkey for us. We're not going to let Thanksgiving go by without roasting a bird."

"You're going to cook?" Kylie looked amazed.

"I'm going to cook. I've developed skills over the past few years you know nothing about."

There was a flash of something primitive in Brock's eyes that connected to something just as primitive in Kylie. With her gaze locked to his, she trembled. The idea of spending Thanksgiving day alone with Brock was scary, intimidating and...exciting.

She shouldn't be feeling excitement now. She should be mourning Alex's loss. She should be nurturing the good memories they'd had between them. She should be remembering their friendship.

But all she could remember was Trish's satisfied expression. All she could feel was the deep betrayal a wife experiences when her husband turns to another woman instead of her.

Underneath all of it was the invisible bond she felt to Brock.

After Gwen and Garrett's visit, Brock had skipped lunch to finish examining the property. As he came into the house that afternoon, he found Kylie washing out her soup bowl.

"You can just leave that in the sink." He wished she'd stop cleaning up after herself. He wished she'd stay put on the sofa, rest and heal. But she wouldn't want to hear that again from him.

To make conversation, he remarked, "Garrett said he used to be FBI." He'd actually enjoyed talking to Gwen's fiancé. They'd quickly established a rapport over computer lingo. Garrett was now a security specialist for Web sites and alarm systems. But mostly, Brock had been interested in his search-and-rescue work. As a pilot, Garrett often took off at the beep of his cell phone to look for a lost child.

"Does Gwen know what she's getting into, marrying a man like him?" Brock asked.

Kylie swung around to glare at him. "What do you mean? He's a good man."

"I don't doubt that. But how does she feel when he takes off in his Skyhawk and she doesn't know when he's coming back?"

"Gwen's strong. And she knows how important Garrett's search-and-rescue missions are to him. She already went through a rough situation with him landing his plane in a snowstorm. That's when they both realized how much they loved each other."

Just from his conversation with her, Brock could tell Gwen was less traditional than Kylie, more assertive and just as stubborn.

"He invited me to the hangar to check out his plane."

"Gwen's dad hangs out there sometimes. He often acts as a spotter for Garrett."

Kylie dried her hands on the dish towel. But as she tried to do it one-handed, the towel slipped through her fingers and fell to the floor. She stooped to retrieve it, but when she came up she wobbled a little.

In two long strides, Brock was beside her, his arm around her, steadying her. "What's wrong?"

"I just got a little dizzy." With his arm around her, she was practically in his arms...practically against his chest...practically holding onto his shoulder.

"You came up too fast," he murmured, his chin close to her cheek.

When she took a deep breath, her hand slipped from his shoulder. He felt the path of it scorch through his shirt. The heat of her body fired his. Remembering that kiss so long ago, he wondered how she'd kiss now that she was a woman.

Damn it, he couldn't go there.

Straightening, he put some distance between them. Only a few inches, but it helped. "Maybe you'd better take a nap this afternoon."

"I don't want to have trouble getting to sleep tonight."

"Then go prop your feet up on the sofa. I can start a fire and you can listen to music."

"I need to go upstairs and finish the beadwork on a Christmas present."

"One-handed?"

"I can use my other hand if I'm careful. I just can't move my shoulder."

"Christmas is still weeks away."

"I have a lot to do. I'm preparing for a baby as well as Christmas. I don't trust myself with a sewing machine yet, but I can work at the table for a little while."

He'd seen the table set up with containers of beads, pieces of leather and special tools.

Wanting to keep an eye on her, he figured out how to do it. "I could start going through the ranch's records while you're there. Then if there's something I don't understand, you could explain it." He wanted to start with the year before his father's death and look at the figures for each succeeding year to see where the money had gone, to examine what expenses had taken their toll, to read why Saddle Ridge had gone into a decline.

"All right. We can do that. I've kept the books since Jack died."

"You have?"

Drawing away from him, she pulled a pack of saltines from the counter and took out a few. "You know Alex always said he didn't have a head for figures."

"I know that's what he said. But I'm not sure I always believed him. He preferred being in the barn to sorting receipts."

"Wouldn't anybody?" she quipped.

"Maybe. Maybe not."

"How about you?" she asked. "Which would *you* prefer?"

"I'd prefer the barn," he replied easily. "But I know reports and vet records and feed expenses all go along with it."

"Alex only liked to do the things he liked to do," she murmured.

There was something in her tone that made him look a little closer. Yes, he saw grief in her eyes, but was there more than that? Had she helped run the ranch into the ground, too? He couldn't see much evidence of that. Still, Kylie could have an expensive hobby he didn't know about besides making Christmas presents for her friends.

"It would be nice if we could just forget the drudgery, but we can't," he remarked.

The statement was meant to be leading, and he waited

for her to say something else. Something more. He wanted to know if the pain in her eyes was from grief and loss or regret. But she didn't say more and the silence weighed heavily between them.

Finally he nodded to the saltines. "I don't see how you can eat those. They taste like cardboard."

"They don't," she protested with a smile. "Especially not when they're fresh. I'm trying to stay away from that chocolate cake Gwen brought."

"She brought it for you to eat."

"Oh, and I'm sure I will. But I'm trying to be good for today. Are you ready to go up now?"

For some insane reason, he wanted to sweep her up into his arms and carry her up those stairs. He wanted to make sure she didn't fall, didn't trip, didn't overuse her shoulder. He was just going to stick close to her for a few days until she was feeling better, yet he realized the thought of doing that was both a pleasure and a pain. When he was around her, he knew he should stay away from her. When he *wasn't* around her, he worried about her. He attributed it all to his big-brother protective instincts taking over. She was such a little bit of a thing, even pregnant.

Had his brother felt this protective of her?

That question gave him a stone-cold feeling. He motioned toward the staircase. "Ladies first."

Once upstairs in the spare room, Brock realized how bad an idea this was. The room was small, barely big enough for the computer setup, Kylie's sewing machine, her craft supplies and the table she worked on. There was a soft leather purse laying on the table with fringes that were partially beaded.

When Kylie sat in the wooden chair at the table, he asked, "Don't you want a pillow or something?"

"A pillow would just slide off. This chair's just right with the table." She switched on an intensity light where she was working.

Although he booted up the computer, that wasn't where his attention stayed. Maybe it was the scent of Kylie's shampoo, or some kind of lotion. She'd never been one for perfume. She'd always chosen natural scents. This combination was something like peach and spice. At least that's what it smelled like to him.

When he glanced at her over his shoulder, she was already busy at work. She had her left arm propped on the table and was using her hands to hold the leather. Her head was bent and her silky, glossy hair, more golden than any wheat field, fell lazily over her shoulder. As she used tweezers and wire, her fingers almost looked as if they were dancing.

Again he turned his focus to the computer screen and the icons there, clicked on the accounting program and found the year he was looking for. But Kylie working silently less than five feet away was a distraction he couldn't ignore.

Out of the blue she asked, "What size turkey did you order?"

"It's big. I just told Vince Shafer to hold one for me. How long has he had the store on Bear Claw Road? He used to sell from his ranch."

Kylie had her lips pursed as she concentrated on slipping the bead onto the piece of rawhide. "Mmm, about three years, I guess. It's only been the last one or two he's gone organic with some of the vegetables. I like that idea, especially now that I'm pregnant." Her gaze came up to meet Brock's and he saw there hopes and dreams and longings that twisted in his chest.

She broke eye contact first and went back to her beadwork.

"How did Alex feel about being a father-to-be?" Brock asked nonchalantly, though he was feeling anything but nonchalant.

She took her time in answering. When she did, it was evasive. "He was getting used to the idea."

"My guess is, he did want a son so he'd be able to teach him all the secrets of bull riding."

After a moment, Kylie responded, "We never really discussed that." Then she stood. "I think I *am* going to take that nap. This position's hurting my shoulder and…and I don't want to make it worse than it is."

When she walked to the door, Brock thought she was as graceful as ever, pregnant or not.

Then she was gone, just like that, leaving him with too many questions.

He was going to find the answers…and soon.

Chapter Three

"Don't even think about it," Brock's deep voice warned from behind Kylie's shoulder.

Thanksgiving morning, coming downstairs and hearing the first floor quiet, Kylie had assumed Brock was outside. He hadn't been around the house much the past couple of days as he helped Dix catch up on chores. She'd gone to the front door, opened it and looked longingly at the barn. That's where she wanted to be.

"I didn't know you were in the house," she replied softly, turning to face him.

"I was washing up. I have an eighteen-pound turkey to wrestle. Remember?"

"I suppose we'd better get it into the oven or it'll never cook through."

"We?" he asked with an arched brow.

"Do *you* know how to make stuffing?"

"You've got a point. I suppose you could oversee and tell me how to do it."

"I know Dr. Marco said to rest for two weeks. But I can't be inactive that long. And I have to get back to work at the temp agency."

"At the end of two weeks, maybe you can *think* about work." He dropped an arm around her shoulders. "You have to learn how to take vacations."

"I've never had a vacation."

When she looked up at him, their gazes locked. His arm was strong and muscled and protective. If he'd meant the gesture to be brotherly, it had failed. She could catch the scent of the soap he'd used from the downstairs bathroom. But he still smelled like hay, too, and a frosty morning. All too easily she got caught up in the moment, forgetting who he was, who she was and why he was here.

He must have remembered. Dropping his arm from around her, he headed to the kitchen. "Tell me what to do first."

She could do that. Or she could clear the air. He was pulling out a chair for her by the kitchen table, but she needed to be on her feet for the next few minutes. "I don't want you to feel responsible for me."

"I *am* responsible for you. You're my brother's wife."

Was that really the way he thought about her? "I have the Warner name. You have an interest in this ranch if I sell it. But you are *not* responsible for my well-being."

The lines on his forehead deepened as the nerve in his jaw worked. Finally he asked, "Why don't you want me here, Kylie, when you so obviously need help? Is it because you think Jack wouldn't approve?"

"Of course not! Jack had no right, ever, to treat you the way he did. He had no right to make you feel as if you should be on the reservation with your mother. He had no right to favor Alex over you." She'd never talked about Jack to Brock this way before, never put all of it into words, and she saw a surprise in his eyes now, as if he believed she hadn't known the depth of what Jack Warner had done to him. How he'd made a small boy feel as if he didn't belong. How he'd pretended Alex was a prince and Brock could leave tomorrow and not be missed.

"And just how would you know about any of that? When you came to live here, I was in college."

"Alex and I went to school together. We were friends. From things he said, I knew what was going on. So did lots of people in town. Wild Horse Junction isn't that big, and Jack was important enough that people talked."

Turning away from her toward the window and the expanse of sugar beet fields and grazing land, he asked, "Why do you think I left?"

"Because your father favored Alex," she answered honestly.

"No. I left because I wanted a life of my own."

"You don't want to be here now." She knew that as well as she knew *she* never wanted to leave.

His expression became unreadable and he wore the stoicism that was so much a part of him. It hid thoughts and feelings and reactions he didn't want anybody else to see. "Whether I want to be here or not isn't the issue. As you said, I have an interest in Saddle Ridge, and I don't want to see it fall into ruin."

"Ruin? That's not what's happening. Once this baby's born—"

"What? You'll train horses day and night? And suddenly all the repairs will be made? The herd will be built up? You'll establish Saddle Ridge's name again?"

Her cheeks were hot, and she felt his questions were a personal attack. "Saddle Ridge already has an established name."

"No, not anymore, and I wonder why that is. Haven't you been schooling horses as long as you've been here? What suddenly happened?"

What *had* happened? She'd analyzed the past five years over and over again.

As if Brock were trying to figure it out, he continued. "Alex was technically good at training cutting horses, even if he didn't have your gift. With the two of you taking clients, breeding stock—" He sliced his arm through the air. "You only have four horses in the barn now. What happened?" he asked again.

She'd never been less than honest with Brock, but she didn't know how to be honest about this. In spite of how Jack had treated them both, Brock had loved Alex, and she knew he was grieving as deeply as she was. But for her, there were other losses thrown in. There was so much more than grief, and she didn't know how to explain any of that. Not without disillusioning Brock. Not without making him more bitter than he already was.

"You might as well tell me, Kylie. I'll figure it out when I get to the last year or two's expenses."

She looked into his bottomless, dark, dark brown eyes, felt the twittering in her belly that wasn't the baby moving and realized her heart was pounding because just being around Brock always did that. Complete silence in the house intensified the tension until it was broken by the wind whistling against the kitchen window.

"It's Thanksgiving, Brock. Can we just enjoy the day without getting into everything?"

Still wearing that cut-in-stone face, a masculine mix of Apache and Anglo, he asked, "Have you become a procrastinator?"

"Maybe I have in some ways. Sometimes reality's easier to face tomorrow."

"What matters is what you do with today."

She gave him her best and brightest smile. "My point exactly. Today I want to stuff a turkey, enjoy the aroma of it cooking, call my mom to wish her a happy holiday, light a fire in the fireplace and think about how my life's going to change with a baby. I don't like confinement, but I'll make the best of it. How about you? How do you want to spend the day?"

She caught a flicker of emotion in his eyes, but it was gone quickly.

"Once we get the bird in the oven, I'm going to exercise the horses and spend a little time with your mustang. We both know, for ranchers, holidays are pretty much like any other day."

"Is Dix going to join us for dinner?"

"No. He said thanks for asking, but after he's finished in the barn, he's heading out to Cody. A friend there invited him to an all-afternoon-and-evening poker party. So it'll just be you and me."

She wanted to ask him how he felt about that. If he'd

rather be anyplace else than here. But that would back him into a corner. He wouldn't want to hurt her feelings, yet knowing Brock, he'd be honest. She didn't want to face that honesty today.

As if proving her point, his gaze fell to her stomach and the baby she was carrying—Alex's child. "I saw the cradle in the bedroom upstairs. Jack had Pete Monroe make it before Alex was born."

"You remember that?"

"I remember a man built like Paul Bunyan hauling it in here. I remember Jack telling him 'that's for my son.'"

There was no evidence now of the boy Brock had been. He'd learned to hide vulnerability. He'd learned to protect himself against his father's lack of respect and attention. But Jack's indifference to Brock had left its mark.

"It's only right Alex's baby should sleep in it," he went on. "I saw you made a cover for the top of the dresser."

"It's padded. I'm going to use that for a changing table. Dix put the bed in the storage barn for me."

"Did you make the decorations on the walls?"

She'd hung one of her smaller quilts in pink, blue and white on the one wall. On the other, she'd arranged a set of nursery rhyme prints that had been a shower gift. "I made the quilt, but a little friend of mine who took riding lessons from me gave me the prints. You'll meet her tomorrow. Her mom's bringing her out for a little while since she doesn't have school."

"How old is she?"

"Molly's ten. She's a great kid. She loves horses almost as much as I do."

"I probably won't be around. I told Dix I'd pick up supplies he needs in town."

Brock was taking care of business, putting Saddle Ridge on the road to recovery. She realized she longed for more. She wanted him to meet Molly and…

Get really involved in your personal life? What will that prove when he's going to leave again? She didn't know.

As Brock took the loaf of bread from the back of the counter to start the filling, she wished she knew what part she wanted Brock to play in her life…in her baby's life.

"Gwen makes a great apple pie," Kylie said lightly after she'd finished her last bite.

She and Brock were sitting on the sofa, eating dessert in front of the fire. She'd tried to keep dinner light, the conversation light, the mood light. They'd been okay as long as they'd talked about Dix or horses. But when their gazes collided, their elbows brushed or their fingers tangled as they reached for the bowl of stuffing at the same time, Kylie knew nothing between her and Brock was light. She was so aware of him beside her, the muscled leanness of his body, his broad shoulders in his denim shirt.

"I'd better put another log on the fire." He'd finished his pie before she had and set the dish on the coffee table. Crossing to the native rock fireplace, he took a log from the fireside basket, moved the fire screen and then settled it into place. With the wrought iron poker he positioned it just right. The flames flared, rose higher and scattered around the log.

Her gaze moved to Brock's back, the fit of his jeans as he crouched, the clean cut of his hair at his nape. She couldn't help making comparisons between him and Alex.

She knew it was wrong. She knew she shouldn't be doing it. Maybe her heart was beating faster every time she looked at Brock because Alex had hurt her so badly.

Never a femme fatale, she didn't have wiles and she didn't play games. Had she been boring to her husband? Had she simply been convenient? Had she been useful? A hard worker? Someone he could count on but not be loyal to? Had she been an absolute fool?

With Brock she felt different from the woman she'd been with Alex. There was something in Brock's eyes when he looked at her that made some of the hurt she was feeling a little less painful.

Yet maybe that's what she just wanted to see. Maybe that's what she *needed* to see.

"When I called my mother, she said she's sending me a Christmas package for the baby," Kylie commented.

"Had you called her after you were in the accident?"

"No. I didn't want to worry her. I told her about it today, though."

"Did she want you to go to Colorado?"

"She's always wanted me to go to Colorado. But I could never live in the city with her and Aunt Marian."

"Does she still work in a department store?"

"Yep. They both do. They share a condo and expenses, and they seem content. My mother was never cut out to be a rancher's wife. I do think she loved my dad, though. When he was diagnosed with lung cancer she talked about coming out here to help me take care of him, and I really think she would have: But then he caught pneumonia, and well, it was too late. I think she always regretted not having a chance to say a last goodbye."

Since she didn't want to go into last goodbyes and what had happened when she and Alex had said theirs, she asked, "How about your mom? How is she?"

"I've tried to convince her to move off the reservation to Houston so she's closer to me. But she says she wants no part of Houston. I don't think it's the city so much as she's afraid to leave what she knows, even if she could have a better life somewhere else."

"She makes jewelry, doesn't she?"

"Yes, she does. She works mostly with silver. She'd love all your beads upstairs."

Kylie had never met Brock's mother. Conchita Vasco Warner had been long gone from Saddle Ridge when Kylie had started school with Alex.

Replacing the fire screen and the poker, Brock sat on the sofa again, and somehow ended up a little closer to her than before. Her arm brushed his, and she looked up at him, planning to say something. Anything. But instead, the depths of his eyes wiped every thought from her head.

"You look pretty today." His voice was low and husky.

She'd sewn the maternity top herself. It was a pink knit fabric with long sleeves and a round neckline. She'd worn it with her expandable jeans. "I'm not sure how you can find me pretty when I'm this fat."

His protest was quick in coming. "You're not fat. That's all baby. And you've got a glow about you." As if he couldn't help himself, he ran his thumb over her cheekbone.

His words were precious to her and she savored each one. "I don't know about a glow," she said with a smile. "But I feel as if I'm…made for motherhood."

There was heat in his eyes now, heat that she was

feeling, too. Behind that heat there was hunger…and need. She recognized it because she knew it. She'd never felt it exactly like this before. It confused her now. Worried her. Upset her. Still, she was curious about it…curious about the vibrations that had always rippled between her and Brock, ever since that year she'd come to live at Saddle Ridge. Even before that on her part. Back then she'd known it was a crush. She'd known he'd never look at her because he was so much older. So much more experienced. When he'd married, she'd realized her crush had been unrequited, one-sided, and she'd better grow up and face reality. She had, and she'd married Alex.

"Why did you divorce?" she asked in an almost whisper.

His expression became guarded. "It was complicated."

"Did you *want* the divorce?"

"I told you it was a mutual decision."

What would Brock say if she told him she'd planned to leave Alex? What would he say if he knew his brother had been unfaithful?

Or were all men just like that? Maybe Brock was like that, too. Something inside her told her he couldn't be. Yet she had to know. There had to be a reason why his marriage hadn't worked out.

"Did she think while you were traveling you were…seeing other women?"

"No. Fidelity wasn't an issue. Not for either of us."

Rising to his feet, he ended the conversation. When he picked up their dishes, she knew he wouldn't answer any more of her questions. Not about his marriage anyway.

Before he could leave the living room, she said, "I had a nice day today. Thanks for cooking. You did a great job."

"I had expert supervision." Then he grew very serious. "I know you think I don't want to be here, Kylie. In a way, I don't. But on the other hand, it was time for me to come back and face a few ghosts."

Face them? Wrestle with them? Win out over them? She had a feeling the longer Brock was here, those ghosts might become less wispy and more real. "How long are you going to stay?"

"Until after your baby's born."

"I won't sell Saddle Ridge, Brock. No matter how long you stay, you won't be able to convince me to do it."

"Even if selling is best for you in the long run?"

"Selling is *not* the best for me or my child."

He considered her pensively. "You could sell off a few sections."

She went quiet, thinking about the money that could bring in.

He took her silence as a rejection of his idea. "You're a stubborn woman."

"Not stubborn, determined. And absolutely certain of the life I want for my baby."

"Life on a ranch?"

"Life on a ranch. On Saddle Ridge."

She had to convince Brock that nothing would make her leave here. She had to convince him she could handle her life on her own.

It wouldn't take much convincing. Once he faced his ghosts, he'd want to wash his hands of her and Saddle Ridge.

Then he'd be gone.

Whenever his eyes filled with heat, whenever his touch

made her heart race, she'd remember that. Brock's life was in Houston. Hers was here.

Heat could never bridge the bitterness, resentment and distance he felt toward Saddle Ridge and Jack Warner that would always be between them.

Kylie was restless, and the cause was simple—she knew Brock was downstairs. Although his presence gave her a sense of safety she hadn't experienced in more years than she could remember, it caused turmoil, too.

She'd remembered to count every one of her blessings today. Thinking back over her life, she knew she was lucky. Her parents had loved her, each in their own way. Her pop had fostered in her her love for horses and the land they grazed on. Although Kylie's mother had left when she was eleven, Kylie had understood her reasons for leaving and had never doubted that her mother loved her. Lynette Armstrong had just gotten sick and tired of a life that could be hard twenty-four hours a day, animals that needed constant tending and a town that didn't have shopping malls. Her mother had met her dad when she'd come to Wyoming on a vacation. They'd fallen in love and she'd stayed. But she'd never felt she belonged, never really *wanted* to belong—not to the life Gus Armstrong was trying to build.

Kylie had often felt guilty she hadn't left with her mother. But of her two parents, she'd felt her dad had needed her more. Not only that, *she* needed the Painted Peaks to fill her soul. She needed the animals to enrich her life. She'd never felt sorry for herself as a kid with only one parent. Maybe that was because Shaye and Gwen had also been her family. She was so thankful for them, too.

When she considered her years with Alex, she felt foolish for believing they could have built a life together. He'd always been a charmer and she'd known that. But she'd believed him when he'd told her she was the only woman he wanted to come home to every night. She'd trusted that his wedding vows meant as much to him as hers meant to her. She'd expected to be Alex's partner in marriage, yet she'd found herself working on it all alone. Still…

Her hand pressed to her belly, and she was so very grateful for Alex's child.

Alex's child.

Whenever she looked at Brock and felt things she shouldn't feel, all she had to do was think about her baby. It was hard enough for one man to accept another's offspring. In Brock's and Alex's case, it would be impossible. Brock's resentment of Jack and Alex and Saddle Ridge had to be immense. Whenever he looked at her, he probably thought about his half brother, the younger son, the one their father had loved.

How could she have such mixed feelings about all of it? How could she be grieving for Alex, but when Brock walked into the room she felt…*touched* in some way? Touched by an excitement, an electricity, a bond that had begun when she was seventeen and had never ended.

Had she loved Alex? Yes, she had. But she had to admit, Brock had always affected her…had always made her heart skip faster.

Her baby kicked and she felt the joy of being pregnant, the trepidation of oncoming parenthood, the certainty that she was going to love being a mother.

"I know who your daddy really was now," she told her

baby. "I know you and I are going to beat this world and make it better for both of us. We can do it on our own. I know we can."

Staring down at her jewelry chest, she thought about everything she still needed for the baby. Thanks to the baby shower Gwen and Shaye had given her, she was in pretty good shape. If she sold another quilt, that should cover the first few months of baby expenses. She wondered if Gwen knew any midwives. A home birth would be less expensive than going to the hospital, and from what she'd read, possibly better for the baby, too. It was time she looked into it.

She ran her fingers over the top of the carved chest. What if Brock stayed until after the baby was born? They each had their privacy, her being on the second floor, him being on the first. But she could hear him moving around. She could hear the water running in the kitchen. She could hear the shower in his bathroom. She could hear the floorboards creak from his heavy bootfalls. Having Brock in the house made her feel safe, yet kept her on edge. That was a contradiction, and she knew it.

Her gaze dropped to the jewelry box once more. It was one of those wooden chests that came from a souvenir shop. Her pop had gotten it for her when she was thirteen. He'd left her alone on the ranch for a weekend while he'd entered a calf-roping event at a rodeo in Montana. She'd been old enough to handle the livestock with Dix, and Gwen had stayed with her for the weekend. When her pop had returned, he'd given her the jewelry chest.

Lifting the lid, she glanced at the pieces of jewelry her mother had sent her for birthdays and Christmas. She didn't wear rings and bracelets much because of working in the barn. And earrings? Her long hair covered them.

The chest had a top layer and a bottom layer. Taking hold of the ribbon on the edges, she pulled up the top tray and set it aside. There in the bottom at the back corner, she found what she was searching for. She'd worn it constantly until the day of Jack Warner's funeral when Brock had brought his wife to the ranch.

Taking hold of the sparkling gold chain, she lifted it. A wild mustang charm dangled from it. Brock had given it to her the night she'd graduated from high school...the night she'd kissed him.

It glittered under the lamp light and brought back memories of the two of them working in the corral with the horses, of Brock tugging her ponytail, of riding the fence line with him to check cattle, of sitting across from him at the dinner table, aware of him in a way she hadn't been aware of Alex.

She'd felt the same awareness today as they'd eaten turkey and stuffing, as they'd sat on the sofa finishing the apple pie.

Her heart hurt. Her throat tightened. And she wasn't sure if she was missing Alex, still feeling stunned by his betrayal, or experiencing nostalgia over a time spent with Brock that was so different from their time together now.

She needed to put it all in perspective.

After clasping Brock's present around her neck, Kylie picked up the cordless phone. Gwen was more likely to be free than Shaye.

She speed dialed Gwen's number. To her relief her friend answered.

"Am I interrupting anything?" she asked quickly.

Gwen laughed. "Interrupting? No. Amy's teething, so Tiffany, Garrett and I are taking turns promenading her around the living room. It's Garrett's turn right now. What can I do for you?"

"The day of my accident I met Alex's mistress."

After a surprised silence, Gwen said, "Tell me what happened."

Chapter Four

By the first weekend in December, the exercises Kylie was doing for her injured shoulder were paying off and she felt much better. The sling was long gone, and as she groomed Feather after breakfast on Saturday, she was pleased the mustang was holding still for her. Not for long periods of time, but long enough that Kylie could run a brush through her mane. She was in the stall with her, alternately feeding her a treat, then running the brush through her flaxen hair.

"Pretty soon you'll let me braid this, won't you?" she asked the mustang.

"Wouldn't it be better if you tied her in the walkway to groom her?" Brock's deep voice asked.

Without looking at him, she explained, "She doesn't like to be tied like that. It makes her jittery."

"You're making *me* jittery being in the stall with her."

"She won't hurt me, Brock."

"Maybe not intentionally."

"We only do this a few minutes at a time." She offered Feather an oatmeal cookie and the horse took it. Then Kylie opened the door that led out to the corral. Feather snickered, swished her tail and made a beeline out, eager to run and play.

"You're spoiling her."

"I'm giving her affection and bonding with her. That's not spoiling."

"What about the homemade treats?"

"It's more economical than buying them."

Brock laughed and shook his head. "I give up."

"Good. Then we don't have to argue."

"Not about that. But I have to wonder why you took on this mustang and added another horse's care to your expenses."

"I *needed* Feather, Brock. That's all I can say. I didn't know I was pregnant when I made arrangements to adopt her."

She exited the stall, closed it and fastened it, then changed the subject. "I went into the tack room this morning for the first time since before the accident. Did you straighten it up?"

"Some."

"And you cleaned the saddles?"

"They needed it."

"Don't think I haven't noticed everything you've done—the repaired porch steps, the coat of paint on the weathered side of the barn. Dix said the riding mower is fixed and—"

"Are you keeping a list?"

"No. But *you* should be. How am I ever going to repay you?"

She did look at him then, and she couldn't decipher the message in his brown-black eyes. There was turbulence there, mixed with anger or something else she couldn't define.

"No repayment will be necessary." His words were terse, his stance rigid and defensive. "I shouldn't have stayed away for so long. I should have come back here to check on Alex…to see how he was handling everything. I never imagined Saddle Ridge would come second to his bull riding. I saw the list of his entry fees and the expenses. Year by year, he entered more competitions."

She felt the need to defend her husband. "He thought he could win money we could pour back into Saddle Ridge."

"He did now and then. I noticed that. But not enough. He wanted the easy fix."

"Bull riding isn't easy."

"Now I know bull-riding was his passion…or maybe addiction. He would have done it whether he won money or not, and you know it."

Yes, she did know it. Bull riding meant more than their marriage. More than her. More than their child. And maybe it wasn't just the bull-riding. It was the lifestyle. Who knew how many women—

As she felt tears prick in her eyes, she turned those thoughts away.

"Kylie?"

"It's hormones," she said, turning away from Brock.

"The hell it is," he muttered, gently clasping her shoulder and nudging her around.

They were standing much too close. Whether it was

logical or not, she thought she could feel the heat of his hand through her jacket and her sweatshirt. He looked so rugged in flannel. His jeans were worn and fit him snugly. Her gaze jerked up to his, and this time she couldn't glance away.

"It's okay to cry," he assured her.

"Crying doesn't help. It doesn't fix anything."

"It releases everything pent up inside of you. You lost your husband a few months ago. Just that, let alone being pregnant, would be enough to handle."

Kylie knew he thought she was grieving over Alex. And she was. But she was grieving over more than his death. She was grieving over lost dreams. She was grieving over the fact that Alex wasn't the man that she'd thought he was when she'd married him. She was also feeling bitterness toward Trish Hammond, and sometimes she almost hated Alex for the feelings she was having now. So the compassion in Brock's eyes just made her feel guilty because she didn't feel like the loving, grieving wife. Yet she didn't want to tell Brock the truth. She didn't want his pity. She didn't want to feel as if she'd failed as a wife.

How had life gotten so complicated?

"Tell me what you're thinking," he prompted.

"I'm not thinking, I'm just feeling...too many things. I can't just spill them out to you, Brock. In some ways I feel as if I've known you all my life. In others, I feel like we're strangers."

He withdrew his hand from her shoulder and then gently he stroked his thumb down her cheek. "We're not strangers."

"If we're not strangers, then why don't I know anything about *your* life?"

"What do you want to know?"

"What's your life like in Houston? How did you feel after your divorce? Have you been dating? What's your five-year plan?"

In the silence, Kylie heard her horse, Caramel, neigh. A bird's wings fluttered high in the barn while cattle lowed in the distance.

"I suppose you don't want one word answers to your questions?"

"With one-word answers, we'd still be strangers."

"Kylie—"

The sounds of a vehicle scattering gravel as it came closer interrupted their conversation. Kylie knew Brock wasn't going to answer her questions now. Maybe not ever. If he did, they'd close some of the distance between them, and she had a feeling he wanted distance there. Maybe for similar reasons that she did.

"Molly's coming to visit again," Kylie explained. Brock had been absent when Molly and her mom visited for a short while the day after Thanksgiving. "She called last night and asked if she could. I invited her to stay for lunch."

"I'll cut out and find something to do in here."

"No," she said quickly, then wondered why she had. "I mean, you don't have to. I'm sure Molly would love meeting you and hearing about some of the places you've been. She's bright, quick and intends to see a lot more of the world than I ever have."

"You've got a long life ahead of you, Kylie. Your world doesn't have to begin and end here." His eyes were intense with the knowledge and wisdom he'd gained over the years.

"I'm going to be busy for the next eighteen years or so," she teased.

"You've got to show your child there's a bigger world. You've got to give him or her the tools to make a life anywhere, not just here."

"I will. But I want my child to know he or she always has a place to belong, always has a place to call home, always has a place that's safe. I want Saddle Ridge to be sustenance and hope and a future."

"Maybe you expect too much. Running cattle now is a lot different than it was a few years ago. The same with breeding horses."

"Are you telling me I can't turn Saddle Ridge around?"

"I'm telling you that maybe you expect too much—of yourself and of everyone else."

Had she expected too much of Alex? Of their marriage? Had she put expectations on him that he couldn't meet, so he'd run away from them? That was a shocking realization to consider.

The side door to the barn opened and Molly ran in, her blond pigtails flying behind her. "Hey, Kylie. I just have to tell Mom you're in here." She ran back to the door and gave a shout.

Seconds later, Molly was beside Kylie, studying Brock curiously.

Before Molly started asking a spate of questions, Kylie introduced them. "Brock, this is my friend, Molly Daily. Molly, this is Brock Warner."

"You have the same last name as Alex and Kylie. Are you related?"

Molly always said what she was thinking, and now Kylie wondered how Brock was going to answer.

"I was Alex's half brother."

Molly studied him thoughtfully. "That means you had one parent the same."

"Yes. Our father."

"Do you like horses, too? Do you ride?" she asked, eyeing him with even more interest.

"I do," he answered seriously, though amusement danced in his eyes.

"With Mr. Warner here, do you think I can take a ride?" she asked Kylie hopefully.

Often, when Dix was around and Molly visited, he watched over her for a few circuits around the corral.

"Mr. Warner might have other things to do." Kylie didn't know what his plans were for today.

"I can spare some time. Which horse do you usually ride?"

"I ride Caramel."

"Caramel, it is. I'll saddle her up."

"She's a good rider," Kylie told him. "She handles herself well on the trail, too."

"We could take a ride over to the first cattle guard," Brock suggested. "That way I can exercise Rambo, too."

Rambo was Alex's horse, a bay gelding that had lots of spirit.

Kylie was a bit surprised at Brock's offer to take Molly out of the corral. She'd only mentioned Molly's ability to trail ride so that Brock knew she could handle herself well. Did he like kids? It would be interesting to see how he related to Molly.

A short while later Kylie watched Brock and Molly lope off. She wandered around the barn a bit, hating her inability to jump right in and muck out stalls, or do whatever needed to be done. Yet she knew her main job right now was taking care of herself so her baby would be healthy.

Finally, sitting on a hay bale and petting one of the cats that roamed the barn, she thought about Brock riding Alex's horse. He sat on a horse as if he belonged on one. She remembered the roundup he'd helped with the summer after her graduation. She'd gone along, too. The group had consisted of Jack, Alex, Brock and two of the full-time hands Saddle Ridge employed then. Gwen had also gone along to keep Kylie company, though she'd admitted she didn't know how much help she'd be. But every horse and rider counted in a roundup.

Brock had stayed away from her. He'd been polite, he'd smiled at her, he'd made conversation when he'd had to. After the roundup was over, he'd congratulated her on a job well done, told her she rode as good as any man and could handle cows and horses just as well. She remembered how wonderful that praise had felt, how much she wanted them to be closer friends the way they had been before graduation. But something had changed that weekend, and she'd blamed it on the kiss.

Kylie was in the tack room folding blankets when Brock and Molly returned. "How was the ride?" Kylie asked.

"Great!" Molly absolutely beamed. "Brock said I'll be as good as you if I keep riding."

"She knows how to sit on a horse," he agreed with a smile.

"We even saw antelope," Molly added with delight.

Antelope were common, speeding across the rangeland, but since Molly lived in town she didn't see them that often.

"Well, I'm glad."

"I know you said you usually help groom, Molly, but why don't you and Kylie go up to the house and set out lunch. I'll take care of Caramel, too."

Molly looked to Kylie for approval, and she nodded, swinging her uninjured arm around Molly's shoulders. "Come on. We'll have everything ready by the time Brock finishes and comes up to the house."

Molly was quiet as they walked up the path. That was unusual for her. She usually chattered a mile a minute.

As they went inside, she said, "Mr. Warner's nice. He told me he's here to help you out."

"Yes, he is. Being pregnant, there are some things I just can't do right now, and Dix has an awful lot to handle."

Both Molly and Kylie washed up in the bathroom, then went to the kitchen to make lunch preparations. Molly was quiet again and Kylie wondered what was on her mind. After Kylie took the beef barbecue from the refrigerator and set it in the microwave to warm up, she glanced at Molly, who was already setting the table.

"You're quiet today," she said simply. "Is something wrong?"

To her dismay, the ten-year-old's eyes filled with tears. Immediately she went to her. "What's wrong, honey?"

"It's just…Mr. Warner was so nice to me."

"Aren't people always nice to you?"

"It's not that. I mean, he treated me like I was his kid or something."

Brock's protective streak made him the type of man who would rescue anyone in trouble. From the way he'd interacted with Molly, she'd also seen he had a knack with kids.

"I don't think Mr. Warner being nice to you is the problem here. What happened?" She didn't want to jump to conclusions that weren't warranted. Molly could simply be upset because a teacher scolded her. Even at her age, she was a perfectionist and she liked adult approval.

"It's just—I don't think my dad loves me." The words came out in a rush, as if they might not be true if she said them fast.

Compassion for Molly filled Kylie's heart. Taking her by the hand, she pulled her over to the table, dragged out two chairs directly across from each other and motioned for her to sit. "Why would you think that?"

"Because he won't…he doesn't…*look* at me. Do you know what I mean? It's like he doesn't want me around. I heard Mom and Dad arguing one night. I don't know what about because I couldn't hear them clearly. But I think they were arguing about *me*."

Kylie didn't know the Dailys well, but what she'd seen of them so far when they'd dropped off Molly or picked her up or when Kylie had seen the three of them together in town, it had seemed to Kylie that her parents had built their world around Molly. Not that anyone truly knew what went on in a family. Didn't *she* know that?

"Tell me something, Molly. How long has this been going on?"

"A few weeks, maybe longer."

"I think I told you how my pop loved horses as much as I did."

Molly nodded.

"Well, he pretty much raised me. My mom went to live somewhere else when I was a little older than you, so it was just me and Pop."

"Did you see your mom?"

"Now and then. But she lived far away. I called her a lot and she called me. I went for visits. She lived in a city, and I couldn't imagine doing that."

"Do you think my parents are going to break up?" Molly sounded horrified.

"Oh, no. I'm not telling you this because I think that. I just meant things were awkward with me and my dad for a while, with my mom not around. And I think part of the problem was my growing up. He didn't know how to relate to me, what to say to me or what to do with me sometimes. I remember the day I told him I needed to buy a bra. He got all red faced and stammered all over the place and didn't talk to me for two days."

"You think Dad's different because I'm growing up?"

"I don't know. Have you talked to him or your mom about this?"

Molly shook her head.

"You should. You don't want to sit and worry over something that might not have anything to do with you."

"You really think it might not have anything to do with me?"

Although that's what she'd said, Kylie knew kids had very good sensors. They could pick up vibrations better than adults sometimes. But she wasn't sure Molly's sensors were working properly. "You won't know until you ask."

"I'll think about it," Molly murmured.

The door opened and Brock came in. Seeing Molly and Kylie sitting and talking in the kitchen, his gaze found Kylie's. "I can find something else to do outside if lunch isn't ready yet."

Kylie shook her head almost imperceptibly, and Brock got the signal. "Lunch is almost ready. The barbecue is warmed up, and after I heat the baked beans and get out the carrot sticks, we're good to go."

Giving Brock a shy smile, Molly hopped up from her chair, went to the refrigerator and pulled out the beans Kylie had made in the slow cooker yesterday.

Brock came to stand beside Kylie and turned to her. When she began to rise, she found his hand under her elbow, helping her up. "How are you feeling? You spent a long time in the barn this morning."

She knew she couldn't just tell him she was fine. He'd already forbidden that. Gazing into his dark eyes, she felt immobilized, as if she could stay there forever. She thought she saw actual concern, more than a sense of duty. Yet she couldn't be sure. She'd never been sure of anything about Brock, except that her feelings for him went deep.

"I got a little chilled, but I'm warming up now."

She saw his expression change as his gaze roamed her face, as it settled on her lips. If she had been chilled from the barn, she certainly was heating up now. Was she reading desire in his eyes? How could she be? She was eight months pregnant, for goodness sakes. He certainly couldn't look at her and think she was attractive. Could he?

"You're getting better at being honest with me." His deep voice was low.

"I've always been honest with you." As soon as she said it, a pang of guilt nudged her. She *had* always been honest with him when he asked her direct questions. But she was keeping things about Alex from him…things that could hurt him.

Then again, maybe he wouldn't care at all that Alex had been unfaithful…that his brother wasn't the man that either of them thought he was.

* * *

As Brock dragged an eight-foot fir from the back of the pickup onto the porch, he muttered a low oath. There were a thousand other ways he should be spending this Sunday. Before snow seriously fell, he had winterizing to do and more painting. But last night Kylie had asked him if he'd cut down a tree for Christmas. She'd also asked him to take her to church this morning.

It had been years since Brock had been inside a church. Although his mother had attended faithfully, his father hadn't been a churchgoing man. Brock had always had too many questions that no one could answer. He found a power bigger than he was in the mountains, in the desert, on a river. Yet standing beside Kylie this morning, hearing her voice raised in song, he'd felt moved by that, too.

He was losing it! That's all there was to it. He knew from experience Saddle Ridge could do that to a man. Especially now, when he was filled with regrets and guilt and grief and a longing he'd forgotten about while he'd lived in Texas.

The door opened and Kylie stood there, a wide smile on her face. It was one of those genuine smiles he'd only seen as she'd gentled Feather and spent time with Molly.

"It's beautiful!"

"How can you tell without setting it upright?" he teased.

"It's big and it's full. That's all that matters."

Suddenly he was glad he'd taken time to choose a tree that had been round, filled-in and well-shaped.

After Brock pulled the tree inside, he saw the boxes of decorations and the pile of Christmas tree lights. "You didn't—"

She cut him off. "No, I didn't. Dix brought everything down from the attic for me. I told him he could help decorate but he didn't seem interested."

"I guess not." Brock wasn't into the idea of decorating a tree himself, but he wasn't going to let Kylie do anything she shouldn't, so that meant he had to oversee.

Realizing a wonderful smell filled the house, he took a couple more sniffs. "What's cooking?"

"Gingerbread."

He'd convinced himself that nothing about Saddle Ridge had changed. The bad memories still had the power to poke him in the gut. However, something *had* changed. Kylie was mistress of the house now, and that made a difference. There was a sense of home about the place that had never been there when he was growing up. Not even after Jack remarried. Carol Warner, Alex's mother, had relied on the housekeeper to cook, had met with her garden society to talk about growing roses, had filled the living room with brocade furniture that Jack had gotten rid of after his wife died. Carol had always been removed from Brock, as if she hadn't known what to do with him. Only Alex had given him a connection.

He still couldn't believe Alex no longer walked the earth.

Was Kylie having trouble believing that, too? Was that the sadness he saw in her eyes? The quietness that was new to her?

Sitting on the sofa, she pulled open flaps of a box that Dix had obviously set there for her.

"Do you use the same decorations every year?" he asked.

"No. There were so many boxes of them, we rotated. Or rather, I did. The boxes are dated." She pointed to the labeling in black marker. "Mostly Dix pulled the older boxes for me, from when you and Alex were kids. I hope that's all right."

"It doesn't matter to me." He imagined she'd had Dix do that so she wouldn't have to confront memories from Christmases with Alex.

As Brock wrestled the tree into the stand, Kylie sorted. "Isn't this pretty!" she exclaimed, holding up an ornament, a silver bell with tiny strings of silver charms dangling from it like a wind chime.

"My mother made that one," Brock said gruffly, amazed at how much wallop an ornament could carry.

"Is it okay if we use it? I think there's more than one."

"I told you, it doesn't matter to me what you use," he snapped, and then was immediately sorry he had. Glancing at Kylie, he expected to see a hurt expression on her face. Instead, he saw compassion, and that was harder to take.

As he concentrated on straightening the tree, he heard her soft footfalls as she came toward him. She was wearing moccasins today. He didn't hear *her* as much as the floor creaking.

"I can use the newer ornaments I collected over the years."

Although he didn't know if he was ready to, he faced her. "I never expected coming back here to be the jolt that it's been. I'd put Saddle Ridge and Jack behind me."

"If your mom made these, I expect she tried to make Christmas the best she could for you while she lived here. It's amazing you even remembered this."

"I was four, and that was the Christmas before my mother and Jack split up."

He was silent as she studied him. "You don't have to

help me decorate the tree. In fact, you don't even have to stay for Christmas. I've recovered now."

"You've recovered from the accident, but you're eight months pregnant. I'm not going to leave, Kylie."

She blew out a breath, and he almost smiled. He imagined she was getting as frustrated with him as he was with her. What a pair!

No, not a pair.

Damn if she didn't look beautiful today. She was still wearing the maternity dress she'd put on for church. It was a red-and-green fine plaid with a high waist that dropped into a calf-length skirt. She'd pulled some of her hair behind her bangs into a beaded barrette. The overwhelming urge to pull her into his arms was so strong, he almost had to physically fight it. In his head he listed all the reasons why he should keep up a wall between them. She'd been Alex's wife. She was carrying Alex's child. She wanted to stay on Saddle Ridge and raise her child, and he wanted to sell the ranch.

"How long has it been since you've seen your mother?" she asked.

"A few months."

"Why don't you ask her to come here for Christmas?"

"Not likely. She wouldn't be comfortable here."

"You know, Jack has been dead a long time."

"Some memories never fade," he insisted. "Why would she want to be reminded of a time in her life when she was unhappy?"

"Maybe she needs to come back here as you did—to exorcize ghosts."

"It's not a good idea, Kylie."

"It was just a suggestion," she said softly, then turned away from him, to go back to sorting ornaments.

After Brock finished setting up the tree in front of the picture window with strings of twinkle lights wound into its boughs, Kylie began decorating it. She'd picked out the ornaments she wanted to use and spread them on the coffee table and the sofa.

He smiled, thinking how organized she was, even in this. To his surprise, she'd apparently also opened one of the later boxes, and he saw many Native American ornaments—a Kokopelli, a white buffalo, a tiny kachina, a storyteller doll. With a miniature mustang in her hand dangling from a red ribbon, he watched as she reached high on the tree. On tiptoes, she suddenly lost her balance.

As though he could instinctually feel what was happening to her, he was by her side, wrapping his arm around her to steady her. The strains of Nakai's Christmas music played in the background as the scent of gingerbread rode on the air. A curious anticipation in Kylie's eyes called to him, and with the vivid recall of a shared kiss in a shadowy barn, he bent his head and set his lips on hers. If he had meant it to be a quick tasting, if he had meant to kiss and quit, if he'd believed he could stay removed and simply satisfy a surface craving, he'd been dead wrong. Kylie was sweetness, passion and all-essential woman. The swell of hunger and need that overtook him demanded a physical reckoning. Thought fled on the wings of the adrenaline coursing through him. He wasn't sure if he breached her lips or if she parted them for him. The vital energy that passed from him to her, and her to him, caught them in an erotic vise.

Kissing Kylie was filled with high sensation—like riding

a mustang bareback through the wind. The exhilaration was heady and intoxicating. His tongue brushing against hers, hers brushing back in response, aroused an appetite he'd never satisfied before. His arm tightened to bring her closer.

Feeling her belly against him, he froze.

The child was between them. Alex's child. Her child. A child that would be blond and blue-eyed and everything Jack Warner had ever wanted in an heir.

Breaking away, Brock kept the fiery words in his head to himself, stunned by the hunger he'd felt for her. He stepped back so their bodies weren't touching. "Forget that happened. We both know it was wrong."

Kylie's eyes were still filled with the haze of desire. "Wrong? That's not the word I'd use. I know what wrong is, Brock, and that kiss wasn't right or wrong. It just was."

"You were Alex's wife."

"Yes, I was. And I'm carrying his child. It's the child that bothers you most, isn't it? Because Alex fathered it. Did you resent Alex so much that you'll stay away from his child the same way you stayed away from him?"

By the way her question came out in a rush, he could tell it had been plaguing her. "I didn't resent Alex. It would have been easier if I had. We were brothers in ways that mattered. But Jack didn't want me here."

"And what about after Jack died?"

"After Jack died, I had a life in Houston, work wherever it took me…and a wife."

There seemed to be so many questions in Kylie's eyes, yet she didn't ask any of them. Instead, she returned to the coffee table and picked up a few more ornaments.

After a slight hesitation, she confided, "I had a crush on

you when I was seventeen. But when you returned to Jack's funeral with a wife, I knew you didn't want me in your life any more than you wanted Saddle Ridge. I think the ranch and me go together in your mind. But if there's an attraction between us, it has nothing to do with Alex. Or with Saddle Ridge. Or with Jack. It has to do with you and me."

He was surprised she'd put her thoughts into words. Of course, he coupled Kylie with Alex! Of course, he coupled her with Saddle Ridge. There was no way in hell he could forget that Alex had claimed her and married her and impregnated her. In his mind, she still belonged to Alex and was off-limits. In his mind, she solidified every reason he'd left and every reason he hadn't wanted to return. As a child, he'd had no choice but to accept his lot as the out-of-favor son. He'd gotten the leftovers that Jack had deigned to throw his way. That night Kylie had kissed him in the barn, he'd known she was too young. He'd known he had to find a life he could be proud of. He'd known he couldn't stand in Alex's way, or he'd lose the younger brother he loved. Then, he'd believed he'd made the right choices. Looking at Kylie now, he wasn't so sure.

He needed cold air and a reprieve from being in the same room with her. "I'm going out to the barn for a while. Concentrate on putting ornaments on the bottom portion of the tree. I'll hang the others for you when I come back in."

The defiant look in her eyes told him she'd do whatever she damned well pleased. Then as quickly as it flared, it dissolved. "I'll be careful, Brock."

As he left the house, he knew she didn't just mean that she'd be careful hanging ornaments on the tree.

Chapter Five

On Wednesday evening Kylie knew she might have made a mistake planning this get-together, but she couldn't handle another evening alone with Brock. Confused and struggling before he arrived, his presence and her turmoil over their kiss blew everything even more out of proportion. She needed her friends, and thank goodness they'd agreed to come—since she agreed to make it a potluck supper, and all she would do was put a roast in the oven.

"It's great," Brock replied to Shaye's question about how he liked the corn pudding. Kylie thought his enthusiasm sounded forced. He'd found himself in the middle of a party, and he didn't like it.

Tiffany, the unwed mother Gwen had taken in, was rocking three-month-old Amy in one arm while she ate dinner. "Kylie said you live in Texas, but you've been all over the world. Did you really ride a camel? And trade your clothes for supplies?"

When Brock glanced at Kylie, she just arched her eyebrows and smiled. Brock had told her a few stories to make conversation during some of their time together, and apparently she'd passed them on.

"The camel was temporary until we could get hold of a Land Rover. And the clothes? I didn't need them, but I did need the supplies. Even in Wild Horse we're used to having a discount store. The closest thing to it in some locales is a weekend flea market. As much bartering goes on as buying."

"Dylan's been all over the world, too," Tiffany informed Brock. "He's even been to Antarctica."

Shaye's husband had been helping Timmy spoon a dollop of mashed potatoes into his mouth, rather than flinging it onto the floor. Kylie knew his nephew—ten months old now—would rather handle it than eat it. "Antarctica, Tasmania, Africa…" Dylan shrugged. "That used to be my life. But I can't say I miss it." He looked over at Shaye sitting on the other side of Timmy.

After she gave a small nod, he went on. "We have an announcement to make."

Before anyone could respond, he held up his hand. "No, we're not pregnant. We'd like a little bit of time to extend our honeymoon before we add to our family. But we have set the wheels in motion to adopt Timmy."

"We want him to have the same name as ours," Shaye admitted. "We don't ever want him to doubt that he's our son in every sense of the word."

"How long will it take?" Kylie asked, as she watched Brock's face.

"About nine months," Shaye replied.

Timmy grabbed a fistful of Dylan's shirt and Dylan laughed. "Another one for the wash," he said easily.

Shaye gave Kylie a conspiratorial wink. "You'd better stock up on soap powder."

"How are the photos going of the wild mustangs?" Garrett asked Dylan.

"I've gotten wonderful shots. I swear, they seem to pose for me. Kylie, Shaye told me you love going to the Bighorns to see them. If you want to ride along with me sometime—"

"I'll take her," Brock interjected. "I haven't been up there in years and I'd love to see them again for myself."

If sitting in a room with Brock was tension-filled, Kylie couldn't imagine the cab of a truck for an hour-long drive.

When Garrett took Amy for a while so Tiffany could devote her attention to her food, Kylie saw he wasn't awkward with the baby at all. When she looked over at Gwen, Gwen's gaze was on her fiancé. There was love and tenderness and hope there. When Garrett glanced back at Gwen, Kylie could just tell that she was his world. They were going to be happy. Truly happy. Just as Shaye and Dylan were. At one time, she'd thought she and Alex could be happy like that, too. But that dream hadn't been based on reality.

Kylie wasn't sure how it happened, but while everyone enjoyed after-dinner coffee except for her, she found herself seated in the armchair. Tiffany perched on one arm, holding Amy. Gwen and Shaye were curled on the floor beside her, while the three men sat on the sofa. Dylan was in the middle with Timmy, Brock and Garrett on the two ends. Conversations split, as they often did when men and women gathered.

With a brush of her long brown hair over her shoulder, Tiffany asked Kylie, "So, do you have a list of baby names yet?"

"No list. I'm hoping that when I look at my son or daughter the perfect name will pop into my head."

"That's one way of doing it," Gwen said with a laugh. "Or...you could just open the phone book and throw a dart."

"I hadn't thought of that," Kylie quipped. "If I get stuck maybe that's what I'll do."

While Shaye and Gwen talked about a new line of baby food and Tiffany went to settle Amy in the car seat she'd brought inside, Kylie heard the men discussing real estate. Timmy, however, was growing restless with the lack of activity. He wanted to be on the floor, crawling. When Dylan wouldn't let him do that, he squiggled around, pushed his little legs and grabbed for Brock's arm.

Brock seemed to freeze for a moment, then visibly relaxed.

"He's looking for a new diversion. He's tired of me," Dylan explained wryly.

Catching Timmy under the arms, Brock admitted, "I've never held a baby."

"There's always a first time. He's squirmy, so hold on tight."

At first Brock seemed awkward as he held up Timmy and let the little boy's feet rest on his legs. But as Timmy waved his arms and grinned his spare-toothed smile, Brock smiled back. "Hi, there. You look as if you're ready to have some fun."

Shaye was paying attention to what was going on on the sofa now, too. "That means putting everything he finds into his mouth, except for food, and that goes on the floor."

Brock chuckled. "It's a big world out there. He has to explore it any way he knows how."

Pushing his little legs against Brock's knees, Timmy bounced up and down. It became a game and the little boy giggled, babbled and drooled.

Shaye rose to her feet. "I don't mean to break up the party, but I've got to go to work tomorrow morning."

Gwen rose, too. "Same here."

As Shaye stood and took Timmy from Brock and Tiffany dressed Amy in her baby bunting, Kylie's guests moved away from her. Except for Gwen, who leaned down close. "Are you really feeling better?"

"I'm doing great. The soreness is almost gone from the shoulder. Brock won't let me lift a finger if he can help it."

"There's tension between the two of you. What gives?"

Kylie had called Gwen the night she had dug out the mustang necklace Brock had given her. She'd ended up telling her about her meeting with Trish Hammond, instead of her turmoil over having Brock in the house. Since their kiss, tension didn't even begin to describe the vibrations between them.

"Brock and I," she murmured, "have a little bit of a history."

Gwen's eyebrow arched.

"I can't discuss it now."

"You don't have to tell me anything. I remember when you were seventeen and moved out here. You spent every moment you could with him."

"I had a crush."

"A crush that's come back to haunt you?"

"No. No crush. Not anymore."

"But something else," Gwen mused, glancing at Brock, who was watching Dylan and Timmy as if no one else in the room existed. Kylie wished she could read his mind.

"Okay. We'll talk later." She clasped Kylie's shoulder. "Don't let what that Hammond woman did influence what happens between you and him."

Kylie knew exactly what Gwen meant. If there was an attraction between her and Brock, it would be easy to salve her ego. When he'd kissed her, she'd never felt so much a woman. Over the past year, she'd doubted Alex's desire for her. She'd doubted how desirable she was at all. Apparently Alex hadn't wanted a woman who'd smelled like horses and hay. He'd wanted a woman like Trish, who smelled like expensive perfume and fine leather.

"I know what you mean," she assured her friend. "Nothing's going to happen. Not with me like this," she said, referring to her pregnancy. "Besides that, Brock will be returning to his life in Texas."

As Garrett brought Gwen her coat, Kylie pushed herself up from the chair. Settling his fiancée's suede jacket on her shoulders, his grey eyes were concerned when he addressed Kylie. "If you need anything just give a yell. We're not that far away. Do you and Brock have cell phones for when he's out mending fence or tending to cattle?"

"Brock has his cell phone. I can always call him from here."

Garrett frowned. "You really need to have one, too. If you're in the barn and you get a cramp or something... I know you probably don't want another monthly fee, but there are temporary cell phones now, the kind that you pay as you go. Just think about it. Okay?"

KAREN ROSE SMITH 97

Like Brock and Dylan, Garrett was the protective type. "Thanks, Garrett. I'll think about it."

After Shaye gave Kylie a goodbye hug and Kylie kissed Timmy's little cheek, Shaye commented, "I can't believe it's less than three weeks until Christmas."

Brock's gaze met Kylie's and she wondered what they'd be doing on Christmas day. She'd already begun knitting him a pair of socks. After she turned in at night, she worked on them for a while. She had to give him something. Hand-knit socks were a small token for all the work he'd done already.

Those socks have nothing to do with repayment for chores that you needed to have done, a little voice scolded her. *You just want to give him something you made for him.*

Being honest with herself, she knew that was true.

After more handshakes and "I'll call yous," Kylie and Brock were alone again.

"You've got good friends," Brock remarked, as he picked up coffee cups and carried them to the kitchen.

Kylie brought along a dish that had held cookies Shaye had made. It was empty. "I'm glad Shaye and Gwen found such good men."

"They do seem happy."

"You sound surprised," she commented.

"I haven't seen many marriages that work. Ten years from now, we'll look at Dylan and Shaye, and Garrett and Gwen and then pass judgment on the institution of marriage."

"You can't go into it thinking it won't work," she offered. "That's setting yourself up for failure."

"No one stands in a church or in front of a justice of the peace expecting to fail."

"I don't know about that. Maybe it's a subconscious

thing. Or maybe we're simply naive. Vows seem easy until they require hard work to make them last." As soon as she said it, she knew she shouldn't have. She didn't want Brock asking her questions.

Instead of asking her questions, though, he seemed to take her words personally. "Sometimes hard work isn't enough."

If she poked into his marriage, he'd want to poke into hers. She wasn't prepared for that. Their kiss had made the subject a more dangerous minefield. Their kiss had changed the way they looked at each other. Their kiss had urged her to keep her insecurities more deeply hidden.

Moving toward the dishwasher, she opened it and began loading it. "Do you know if Dix cut pine boughs for me today? Tomorrow I'd like to work on wreaths. One for Gwen and Shaye and one for us."

"For the front door?" he asked.

She straightened and nodded.

"You always did like tradition," he said in a gruff voice.

"Tradition can get us through some difficult times. After Mom left for Colorado, Pop and I had to come up with our own traditions so we weren't so sad over the ones Mom had liked. We couldn't do the same things because that would have hurt too much. In the years I went to Colorado to spend Christmas with Mom, she and Aunt Marian had come up with their own traditions. I think they're just our way of having something to hold onto, something to share that's familiar."

"I suppose you and Alex had traditions," he suggested offhandedly.

After a moment, she replied, "I'm not sure if you had asked Alex what they were if he would have known."

"He couldn't have told me you always put a wreath on the door?"

"I think he took it for granted, so he really didn't see it, just like Christmas cookies and cranberry bread and tinsel on the tree."

Brock glanced at the fir. "We didn't put tinsel on the tree."

She avoided his gaze. "I know. I wanted it to be different this year."

"Whether it's different or not, you're going to miss him. You don't have to hold it inside when you're around me. I understand."

What he didn't understand was that her marriage had been falling apart and she hadn't been able to save it. But she had too much pride to tell him that. Failure wasn't something she accepted easily. The fact that she'd failed at the most important thing in her life was most upsetting of all.

The silence that fell between them was like a curtain separating them. Finally he broke the stillness. "New traditions remind us that old ones still mean a lot. You can change what you do, but you can't forget what you *used* to do. At least most people can't."

"I'm going to try." This discussion was over for tonight. It might be over forever.

Because they were getting too close to truths Kylie didn't want Brock to know.

When Kylie entered the ranch house Saturday afternoon around three, she didn't expect Brock to be there. But there he was, sitting in the kitchen, a lockbox in front of him on the table. She didn't recognize it.

Before she could find out what he was doing, he asked, "How was your lunch with Shaye and Gwen?"

Although he'd asked the question, she wasn't sure he really wanted to know. "It was great. The Silver Dollar wasn't busy, so we had time and quiet to talk."

Gwen had picked her up and then dropped her off so Kylie didn't have to drive. But she didn't like being chauffeured. She didn't like not being completely independent. After her doctor's appointment on Monday, she'd go back to work and be her own person again.

Brock's gaze fell to the grey metal box on the table. "I found this in the bunkhouse in one of the closets, way in back on the floor."

"What is it?"

Brock wasn't quick to answer. When he did, his expression was more sober than she'd ever seen it. "I believe it was Alex's secret stash."

Although the lid was open, she couldn't see into the box from where she was standing. "Money?"

"No." Standing, Brock pulled out a chair for her. "I think you'd better sit down."

"You're scaring me." She felt cold all over.

"I don't mean to scare you. Come on, take off your coat."

He helped her with her parka. The brush of his hand on her shoulder warded off some of the sudden chill. As she lowered herself into the chair, he hung the coat on a peg on the wall.

"No one's stayed in the bunkhouse for two years," she murmured.

"Alex knew that. That's why he put this there. No chance of anybody finding it." Taking out a sheaf of credit card bills, Brock placed them on the table in front of her. "Did you know Alex had a Visa card in his own name?"

She and Alex had had joint credit cards—a Discover and a MasterCard. The MasterCard they'd used strictly for ranch purposes.

"No, I didn't know that." Then something occurred to her. "How could he? No statements ever came to the house."

Brock's finger went to the address on top of the page. "They went to a P.O. box."

"I didn't know he had a P.O. box."

"Do you have Alex's wallet and keys?"

When she would have stood to go get them, Brock laid a hand on her shoulder. "Just tell me where they are."

With her mind racing, her stomach twirling, she pointed into the living room. "In the right bottom drawer of the writing desk."

The piece of furniture was an antique. There were two small drawers. The top part opened and lay flat on two braces that slid out to support it.

Quickly Brock went to the drawer and removed a key ring with about a dozen keys, as well as a worn, brown leather wallet.

"Did you go through his wallet?" he asked gently, as he sat beside her once more.

"Yes, I did. But it was right after he died and I guess I was distracted." Actually, she'd sat and cried as she'd gone through it. He'd had lots of cards—two credit cards, a phone card, an auto club card, an ID card, a charge card for the Trading Post in town. Now, as she sorted through them she saw the Visa card. Why hadn't it jumped out at her before?

Because her mind hadn't been on credit cards. It had been on mementoes—things he might have had in his wallet that had meant something to him. Or to her. In one of the flaps she'd found a bootmaker's business card, as well as a parking receipt for his last rodeo.

"You've never seen the credit card before?"

She shook her head.

Picking up the ring of keys he asked, "Do you know what each one of these goes to?"

She'd taken his truck keys off the ring. There were two for the house, a set for her pickup that had been in the accident, small padlock keys that she had duplicates of that opened sheds. She didn't know anything about the last three. Suddenly she wondered if one of them opened Trish Hammond's apartment.

Brock focused on one that wasn't as large as a house key nor as small as a padlock key. "I think this goes to the P.O. box. The number's on it."

She was less concerned about the P.O. box than the bills before her. It looked as if Alex had paid the minimum most months, letting the two-thousand-dollar balance stand. Did she owe two thousand dollars more? she wondered.

When her eyes sped down the list of expenditures on each bill, that cold feeling returned…so cold that she almost dropped the paper in her hand. The list of purchases ranged from flowers and candy to a five-hundred-dollar gold bracelet and charges for hotel rooms. She could feel Brock's attention on her, and she didn't know what to do or to say. She'd known Alex had cheated on her with Trish. How many others had there been? Did she even want to know?

"Did you know he was cheating on you?"

There was an edge to Brock's voice and an inflection that said he was angry or disappointed or...something.

Raising her chin, she looked right into his turbulent brown eyes. "Our marriage was in trouble. He was away so much and I thought that was the real problem. I had gotten hang-up calls, but I didn't really know for sure what was going on until—until the day of the accident."

"The bull-riding accident?"

"No. *My* accident."

"But Alex had been dead almost four months."

"The woman he'd been seeing called me, supposedly about boarding a horse. Trish Hammond is a waitress at Clementine's, and I met her there after work. After I got there, she took out a belt buckle that Alex had given her in April. She said she thought I might like to have it, but she just wanted to see my reaction. She wanted to see me upset. She wanted me to know she was the other woman."

"I don't understand why she'd do that."

Kylie shook her head. "I don't, either. I guess she just wanted to see me suffer more. Or else she was curious as to who I really was. I didn't say much. I was really upset. As I was driving home, that's when the ball joint broke."

The moments ticked by, and she knew Brock was waiting for the whole story or anything else she was willing to tell him. "When I found out I was pregnant—" Her throat tightened.

"I knew it wasn't the best time, but I wanted this baby. Alex didn't. He thought I'd gotten pregnant just to trap him into staying home more. We argued, and I told him if he didn't go to counseling with me, I was going to leave. He left for Las Vegas early, and that was the last I saw him. I wish...I wish so many things had been different." She stopped then because the lump in her throat was too big, her sadness too great, her regret too overwhelming at that moment.

When Brock reached out and took her hand, the tears crept loose and she shut her eyes.

Taking a deep breath, she swiped away the wetness. She didn't want Brock's pity. "You must think I'm just another weak woman who couldn't face the truth."

"That's not what I think at all. You're strong, Kylie. I've always known that. From the time you were running your pop's ranch with him, everyone in town knew nothing could keep you down. You wanted your marriage to work and nobody can fault you for that."

She had desperately wanted her marriage to work. She'd believed in her vows made before God. "When I married Alex, he needed me. We'd always been such good friends. We'd both lost our dads, and I thought we understood each other. I think he liked the idea of marriage, but *being* married was something else. I've lain awake at night wondering what I could have done differently. Maybe I shouldn't have taken on so much of the responsibility. Maybe I should have gone with him to more of his competitions. Maybe I should have prettied myself up so he didn't look elsewhere."

Brock made some kind of noise and she saw the nerve in his jaw work. But he didn't say anything, and she had no idea what he was thinking. He was still holding her hand, though, and that felt good and safe and secure…and right.

Yet how could it be right when so much else was wrong?

"I'm just beginning to see that you've been carrying too much of the burden for too long," he said. "I want you to call Mr. Tompkins and tell him you're not coming back to work."

"Brock, I need the money."

"No, you don't. You need to take care of yourself and your baby. The little bit of money you're going to bring in in the next six weeks or so isn't worth the cost to your health or the baby's. Can't you see that?"

"I see that I have bills to pay."

"You're not the only one with regrets. I should have kept in touch with Alex better, especially after Jack died. I should have seen what he was doing and how he was treating you. So this is what's going to go down. You can sell off a parcel of land on the north border. That'll give you capital. If it's not enough, I'll add some to it. And I'll come up with a plan. It'll take a couple of weeks until I figure out what's best to do. But by the time I leave here, you'll be up and running again."

Mixed emotions battered Kylie. Gratitude warred against pride. "I hate the idea of you rescuing me."

"I could be insulted." His eyebrows arched and his lips twitched with amusement.

"If I let you do this, I'll be indebted to you."

"No. I'll be indebted to *you*. You've managed to keep this place, Kylie. For all Alex did, the bank could have foreclosed."

"If you put your own money in, then you deserve a share of the profits."

When his eyebrows furrowed deeper, she said, "I mean it, Brock. I won't take a handout. I won't be a charity case."

"You're not one."

"Well, I feel like I am."

"All right," he agreed, relenting. "I'll accept some profit. We'll figure out something. But we'll put a moratorium on it, too, until the ranch is in full swing again."

"How long a moratorium?" she asked warily.

"A year."

"Six months."

"Kylie, it's going to take that long just to figure out what will work and what won't."

"Six months. I'll be able to send you something regularly by then. I know I will."

"I don't know if you're the most optimistic woman I've ever met, or just the most determined."

"With a child to think about, I have to be both." She looked down at the credit card statements. "I can't believe he kept all this from me. I can't believe I was so naive."

"I'm not sure naive has anything to do with it. You wanted to believe the best of Alex. You wanted to think your marriage was sacred. So did I. It's ironic, but my breakup had to do with children, too."

"Your wife got pregnant?" The idea of that challenged Kylie's equilibrium. She definitely didn't like the idea of another woman pregnant with Brock's child, though she had no right to object to that. No right at all.

"No, she wasn't pregnant, and that was the problem. Maybe Alex and I weren't so different in some ways. After we were married a year, Marta wanted to have kids. I didn't."

That didn't seem to jive. Brock would make a terrific father. She'd seen that with Timmy and with Molly. "Why didn't you want children?" she asked gently.

"I could tell you the time didn't seem right, that I knew I'd be away from home a lot, that a child would tie us down when we were making advances in our careers. But the real bottom line reason went much deeper. It went back to Jack marrying my mother, looking at me when I was born and wanting something different. You saw Marta. Tall, sleek, light brown hair, porcelain skin. Just what would have happened if our baby had been born with a broad face and black eyes? How would she have felt then?"

"Did you ask her?"

"I did. She said she was sure our child would be a mixture of both of us."

"So what happened?"

"I wanted to keep the marriage intact. I agreed we'd try to get pregnant. We moved from a condo into a house and I didn't take foreign assignments. But when we didn't get pregnant, we began growing apart. Finally, we saw a specialist and were both tested. Everything was fine. She blamed me. She said I didn't really want a child and that was a subconscious barrier."

He stopped and blew out a breath. "To show her I was invested in the decision, I went along with trying artificial insemination. That didn't work, either. I thought we needed a break from all of it, and I suggested we take a vacation and just relax. But her idea of relaxing and mine were very different. We decided to take a cruise so we could have a little bit of everything. But on the ship, we didn't have the same interests. We found ourselves going our separate ways. When we came back together at night, we didn't have much to say. She wanted a baby. That's *all* that was on her mind. When we got home, she asked for a divorce. She wanted to start over before it was too late to do it with someone who wanted a family as much as she did."

"Oh, Brock. I'm so sorry. You must have felt so betrayed. Wedding vows mean taking the bad with the good, riding it out when it doesn't look like you can. I still believe if Alex had gone to counseling with me we could have turned our marriage around. But we both had to be willing to try."

"We both got the raw end of the deal. But at least Marta was honest about what she wanted. Alex…Alex was spoiled and pampered and thought he always had to get his own way. Jack did a disservice to Alex by letting him think the world revolved around him. I knew it didn't. I knew I had to cut my own path. But Alex expected everyone to just hand over whatever he wanted."

"They usually did," Kylie admitted without bitterness. "He had this way about him that just—" She stopped, overcome by what she once felt, overcome by pain that it had all gone so wrong, overcome by the concern that she was lacking and always would be. She knew she was to blame in this, too. She should have *been* more…*done* more. If she had been the best kind of wife, Alex wouldn't have looked elsewhere.

As if Brock heard the thoughts running through her head, he stood, then took her hands and pulled her up with him. "Don't blame yourself for the failure of your marriage."

"It was my fault as much as it was Alex's. Don't tell me you didn't blame yourself."

"My situation was altogether different. Alex was the type of man who needed adulation. He needed the crowds cheering for him when he rode that bull. He needed women looking at him as if he was God's greatest gift. *Women.* Plural. Not just you. Alex was always like that. I thought marrying you would change him. But apparently, marriage didn't have any affect at all. I'm sorry about that, Kylie, because you deserved better."

"Whatever my marriage to Alex was or wasn't, it gave me the greatest gift of my life." Her gaze lowered to the child she was carrying. Then she looked up at Brock again. "I have to believe that if Alex had lived, he would have learned to become a dad. Even if I had left, I would have always encouraged that. You said you thought our marriage would change him. It didn't. But I do believe having a child would have. Being pregnant has changed *me*. It's made me stronger, more sure of the life I want to lead, more aware that I have to make right decisions."

"You've grown up," he said, sounding as if he might be surprised by that fact.

Because she and Alex were the same age and Alex had never grown up? "I think part of me has always been grown up."

His eyes grew darker, almost black. The light there was full of heat. She felt it, connected with it, wanted more of it.

Be careful, her common sense warned her. *You're vulnerable,* it went on. *You're susceptible.*

The thing was, she'd always been susceptible to Brock. Now she wondered if her crush had been more than a crush.

Instead of drawing her closer, touching her or kissing her, Brock dropped her hands. "I'm going to go into town and check if there's anything in that P.O. box. I'll bring home a form so you can have mail forwarded to here."

What if she told Brock she wanted to go with him? That was silly. A ride into town would accomplish nothing. She had so much to do here, and she'd better get to it.

She had better not wrap her old feelings for Brock into a new package. A baby was between them. Her marriage to Alex was between them.

That would never change.

Chapter Six

On Tuesday evening Kylie walked into the veterinary clinic a little less defiant than she'd felt that afternoon when she'd left for work. Yesterday her doctor had given her the okay, both to work and to drive. Brock and Dix both were acting like her keepers, disapproving of her doing either. But she was determined to maintain some semblance of independence.

She wasn't disregarding their concern or her own well-being. She had arranged a schedule with Mr. Tompkins that took the end of her pregnancy into consideration. The office would be closed between Christmas and New Year's. He'd found someone to replace her as of January fifteenth. Until then, his wife, who had been filling in the last couple of weeks, would work mornings and Kylie would work in the afternoons. This way she wasn't leaving him in the lurch, could earn some extra money, yet also was looking after her health and the baby's.

In the clinic's waiting area, one man held a black Lab by his leash while the dog snoozed at his side. The woman sitting a few feet away from him held a carrier on her lap and Kylie glimpsed a tortoiseshell long-haired cat inside.

The receptionist, Sherry Watson, smiled at Kylie as she approached the desk. "I'm here to pick up Molly. Is she in the back with Dr. Buchanan?"

Dr. Seth Buchanan was Molly's uncle, and the ten-year-old enjoyed spending time at the clinic whenever she could. She not only liked horses but furry creatures of all kinds, and Kylie suspected the little girl might become a veterinarian herself someday.

"Molly's mom told me you'd be stopping by for her. Going Christmas shopping, I understand."

"That we are. She wants to find the perfect gifts for her parents and can't do that when they're around."

Sherry lowered her voice conspiratorially. "Dr. Buchanan said something about giving her a bonus for helping him. Molly was all smiles because she said now she could afford to buy her mom a new pair of leather gloves."

"Then I guess we'll be stopping in at Tannenbaum's Leather Shop."

"Do you want me to get her?" Sherry asked.

"No, I'll just go on back." Seth had doctored the Warners's horses for the past six years, ever since he'd returned and taken over running the clinic from his father, who had retired.

Kylie found Molly sitting on the floor in front of the kennels, playing with a Cocker Spaniel pup. She was holding one end of a rope, the pup was holding the other, and they were occupied in a pretend tug-of-war. She looked up when Kylie opened the door and slipped inside.

There were ten cages. Only one was occupied right now by a sleeping yellow tabby.

Seeing Kylie's gaze go to the cat, Molly explained, "She was spayed this morning. Her owner's coming to pick her up in a little while."

"And who's this?" Kylie asked, motioning to the pup.

"She doesn't have a name yet. Uncle Seth says he's looking for a good home for her. Somebody just left her here. He doesn't know who."

The pup suddenly lost her grip on the rope and fell back on her hind quarters, then plopped over on her side, looking up at Molly with big brown eyes.

"I'm thinking about asking Mom and Dad if they'll get her for me for Christmas. But they…"

Kylie waited.

"I think they were fighting again this morning. They got all quiet when I came down for breakfast." Picking up the pup with one hand, Molly plopped her into her lap and scratched her behind the ears.

Kylie didn't want to butt into something that didn't concern her, yet Molly was obviously upset about her parents.

"Do you think you're ready for the responsibility of a dog? If she's yours, you'll have to take care of her all the time, not just when you want to."

"I'm ready. She could be my best friend. She could even sleep with me. Then I wouldn't feel so…alone."

"If you don't want to bring up the subject with your parents, maybe your Uncle Seth could."

"That's a great idea," Molly said, brightening. "And since he's mom's older brother, she'll listen to him."

Suddenly the door to the kennel opened, and Seth Buchanan stepped inside. He was six feet tall, with dark brown hair and blue eyes and a friendly smile. "Hi, there. I'm between patients. Sherry said you came to pick up Molly. I heard you were in an accident. How are you doing?"

"I'm good. All recovered now. Just waiting for the baby."

"How's Feather?"

"She's great. Come spring, I'll really be able to work with her."

"Brock was in last week for ointment for one of the horses. I understand he's been working with Feather, too."

"You and Brock know each other?"

"Sure. I used to tag along with my dad when he made ranch calls. I was a couple of years older than Brock, but that didn't seem to matter much. We fished together plenty of Saturday afternoons."

Kylie heard footsteps outside the kennel. When she looked through the panel of glass, she saw Sherry showing the woman with the cat carrier into one of the examining rooms.

"It looks as if Tango is ready for her rabies shot," Seth commented.

Kylie grinned. "Tango?"

"I don't name them, I just treat them."

While they were talking, Molly had picked up the pup and settled her back in her cage. "Can I talk to you for a minute, Uncle Seth?" she asked.

He checked outside and then looked back at his niece. "Sure."

Kylie said to Molly, "I'll wait for you in the reception area."

As she opened the door to head that way, Seth called, "You take care. If I don't see you before, you have a good holiday."

Kylie saw the compassion in his eyes, and she knew he knew the holiday would be hard for her. Sometimes she still couldn't believe Alex was gone. It just seemed as if he were away, and he'd be walking in the door again anytime. A lump formed in her throat and she couldn't help the tears that came to her eyes.

Blinking rapidly, she just nodded at Seth, and said, "You have a good holiday, too," then escaped out to the waiting area where she could compose herself before she took Molly to the leather goods store.

A half hour later, Kylie stood beside Molly at the cashier's desk, watching the little girl count out her money. With her uncle's bonus, she had just enough saved to cover a pair of gloves for her mom that were on sale and a wallet for her dad.

When the buzzer above the door announced a new customer, Kylie looked that way and was stunned to see Brock. He came toward her, a cautious expression on his face, and she knew that was because this meeting was no accident.

"Let me guess," she said as he approached her. "You had this sudden, overwhelming need to buy a new belt."

"Actually, I need a coat to keep me warm through a Wyoming winter."

"And you just happened to decide today was the best day to buy it."

"I stopped at the clinic. Seth said you were headed this way." When she continued studying him relentlessly, he admitted, "It was your first day back at work. I wanted to see how it went."

"I would have told you when I got home."

She was giving him no quarter and he began to look exasperated. "All right. I suspected you'd be tired after working and shopping, you wouldn't want to cook, and you might appreciate supper at the Silver Dollar. That's all."

Her attitude softening a bit, she commented, "And since we'd have two vehicles, you'd just follow me home." She did really like the new truck he'd bought her. It had all the latest gadgets.

"You seem to have all the answers." His voice was dry.

"No, just the obvious ones." The truth was, his protective streak made her feel cared for. Alex had never done anything like this. Never tried to be protective. Never tried to keep her safe.

She *had* to stop comparing.

Even if Brock was looking after her out of a misguided sense of responsibility, she did appreciate it. It just took some getting used to.

"Molly and I were going to stop in at Flutes and Drums. I finished another beaded purse for Lily to put in her display case."

Flutes and Drums was the gallery that carried Dylan's photographs and prints, as well as other artists' works. Lily had been carrying Kylie's beaded coin purses for the past year, and that brought in extra money, too. Tourists were willing to pay exorbitant amounts for hand beading. This time of year, Lily sold them in the gallery as well as on her Web site.

"You two go ahead. I really do want to check out the sheepskin coats."

"And what will you do with that once you're back in

Houston?" She had to keep reminding herself he wasn't going to stay.

"I travel to cold climates. It'll come in handy then."

Always ready with an answer, Brock didn't do anything without good reason. That aspect of his personality hadn't changed.

Glancing over at Molly, Brock saw she was engaged in conversation with a clerk. They were discussing the snakeskin boots behind the counter and how much they cost.

"Seth was concerned about you when you left. He said he mentioned the holidays and you choked up."

"It's hormones."

"I think we both know better than that."

"I'm okay, Brock. Really."

His frown deepened. After a few seconds, he asked, "Are you and Seth good friends?"

That question had come out of left field. "He's been taking care of the Warner horses for years."

"That's not what I asked."

She saw something in Brock's eyes then that she didn't like. She didn't like it at all. Because she knew exactly what he was thinking. "Seth is the veterinarian who takes care of Saddle Ridge's horses," she told him flatly. "And I think I just changed my mind about having dinner with you. I'll get home on my own just fine."

When she would have turned away from him, he caught her arm. "Kylie, I wasn't accusing you of anything," he assured her in a low voice.

"Weren't you?" Her words were almost a whisper. "Did you think because Alex was gone so much I tried to find other company? Well, I didn't. The horses were my company. Seth is a friend who cares about what happens to me. That's all."

"You put up with a lot from Alex, and it would only be natural to turn to someone."

"I turned to Gwen and Shaye. I don't need a man to comfort me...or to define me."

Still, Brock didn't release her. "You asked me the fidelity question, Kylie. Why is it so different when I ask you?"

All at once, she realized she expected Brock to know her, to trust her, to automatically believe she was telling the truth. Alex had betrayed her. Brock's wife had walked out on him. She had no right to be judgmental or self-righteous.

She sighed. "Molly and I will meet you at the Silver Dollar in about twenty minutes. Is that all right?"

Brock's gaze was intense as he nodded, then moved away to examine sheepskin jackets.

Kylie's heart beat faster as she joined Molly at the cash register, finally understanding that she and Brock didn't know each other at all.

Brock hung his hat on the caddy in the kitchen, not knowing how he was going to stay at Saddle Ridge until after Kylie delivered her baby. Every time he turned around he bumped into a memory, most of them bad. Besides that, when he looked at Kylie, he wanted things that could never be. All *he'd* ever wanted to do was escape Wild Horse Junction. All *she'd* ever wanted to do was put down deeper roots.

Tonight, he knew he'd hurt her. Although she'd asked a question aimed at him about fidelity, questioning *her* was somehow different. He wasn't sure why or how. It just was. Because of that, their meal had been anything but companionable.

He hung the new, sheepskin jacket on the hook under his hat and waited for Kylie to remove her parka. When she did, she avoided his gaze and he knew he had to confront what had happened. "Tell me what you're thinking." It was more of a demand than a request, and he half expected her to get defensive.

Instead, she took a lighter tack. "Most women don't think in the linear, one-track fashion. What I'm thinking at any moment can get very messy."

Taking her coat from her, his fingers brushed hers. The immediate, sharp jolt that forked through him had nothing to do with static electricity and everything to do with what had always been between the two of them—an attraction he'd constantly denied.

After he hung her jacket beside his, he said disapprovingly, "You're being evasive."

"I'm being truthful."

With a frustrated, exhaled breath, he dug his hands into his front jeans pockets. "You want me to apologize."

She didn't pretend she didn't know what he was talking about. "No, that's not true. I didn't want you to have to ask the question in the first place. Did you think I could be carrying Seth's child instead of Alex's?"

He couldn't deny the thought had passed through his mind.

Kylie shook her head, her hands fluttered in front of her and then she turned and went into the living room. He followed her and caught her before she could go up the staircase into her bedroom and shut him out.

"What did you think I was going to do?" she asked, her voice catching. "Pretend this baby belonged to Alex when it didn't? Brock, for goodness sakes. Are you so cynical that you'd believe I'd be that deceitful? Would I even care about Saddle Ridge if I were in love with another man?"

"It's a valuable piece of property." He knew he was playing devil's advocate now and he didn't know why he was doing it.

"I worked so hard to keep Saddle Ridge going so Alex and I would have a future. So we'd have a family who could have a future."

"I was jealous," Brock finally admitted.

Her eyes widened in surprise.

"Jealous that Seth had a proprietary air toward you. That he knows who you are now, and I don't. He has a genuine affection for you that made me wonder if he was going to move in now that Alex is gone."

"Move in?" She was struggling to understand what he was thinking.

"Not move in literally. But move in...get friendlier, suggest dinners, bring the baby presents, move into Alex's place. Or fill the spot Alex never could...or would. Why wouldn't you turn toward a stable, caring guy like Seth after what Alex put you through?"

She sank down onto the sofa murmuring, "And I thought *I* had a messy thought-life."

If this conversation weren't so damn serious, he'd have to smile. He dropped down beside her, wishing he'd never gotten involved in this discussion...wishing he'd never asked the question in the leather shop.

"I've always thought you were beautiful. That weekend

after your graduation, you kissed me and I responded. I shouldn't have. You were too young. I was too old."

"You're only five years older than I am."

"Back then, that made a big difference. You and Alex were the same age. That weekend, he told me he was going to marry you."

"He *what?*"

"I figured the two of you already had something going…that when you kissed me that night, you were grateful for the gift, and I responded to a kiss like any man would."

"Alex and I didn't have anything going. I'd never even kissed a man before that night."

Now he was truly shocked. "You and Alex had been friends all of your lives."

"Yes, *friends*. We got really close after your dad died. After…" She hesitated a moment. "After you came back here married."

What could he say? That their timing had been off? That everything would have been different if he hadn't gotten married? That everything would have been different if he would have pushed aside Alex's wishes and his desire to marry Kylie? Even so, Brock still didn't think anything would have changed. She had still been too young for him, or he had been too old for her. He'd wanted a life away from Wild Horse Junction. He'd wanted a career that would set him above being a rancher. He'd wanted to make his mother proud and her dreams come true. And *his* dreams? They weren't defined back then. They weren't defined now. Kylie's were, and he admired that about her.

At least his dreams hadn't been defined until this moment. Realizing dreams were wispy images that were elusive, he let real desire rush through him. Reality could be better than a dream. Grasping here and now seemed so much more important than the future.

Kylie's blue eyes were filled with questions, and maybe even anticipation. He knew her feminine ego had been wounded badly by Alex's betrayal. More than anything, he wanted her to know she was a beautiful, desirable woman. Her hair was long and silky and slid across her shoulders whenever she moved. Her bangs were long, touching her eyebrows—eyebrows that were honey-colored, darker than her hair. For as long as he'd known Kylie, he'd never seen her in full makeup. A touch of lipstick was all she ever wore. Now only the slightest coating of it remained, making her lips slightly pinker than they would be naturally. He was more aroused than he wanted to admit, just looking at her…just thinking about kissing her.

"Brock." His name was a whisper and consent to an unasked question.

"If I kiss you again, we're both going to regret it."

"Are you so sure?"

No, he wasn't sure. His life was twisting and turning and changing. So were his intentions, his thoughts, his memories. And his dreams. Whereas he once knew exactly what he wanted, now his goals seemed nebulous. His divorce had made him throw more attention into his work. He'd focused on the parts of his life he could do something about—earning a living, saving for retirement, doing the best job he could for anyone who hired him, putting in long days so he'd sleep at night, stowing his sex drive in the deep freeze because he didn't want a one-night stand or the complications of a relationship.

Now that sex drive was fully awake and raring to go. Cor-
ralling primitive tendencies that could get way out of hand,
he forced himself to concentrate on Kylie. When he lifted her
chin and traced his thumb over the soft point, her lips parted.
Still, he didn't hurry, didn't command, didn't take. Rather,
sliding his hand to her cheek, he held her gently, leaned in,
then finally let his lips brush hers. Lips on lips, yearning cut
so deep inside of him, he felt as if a horse had kicked him in
the stomach. But then pure adrenaline shot through him. As
Kylie's softness tempted him, he was remembering how
deeply a man could need and how hungry a man could get.
Kissing Kylie took him to a place where the wind blew,
where mustangs roamed free, where water fell over cliffs and
sunlight glazed the world in a glorious glow.

Their mouths opened. Their tongues questioned and
then quested, took and then received, satisfied and taunted.
He couldn't get enough, and she couldn't seem to, either.
They went deeper, longer, wetter, until his hand slid from
her face to her breast and he held it in his hand. Her breasts
were fuller since her pregnancy and that fullness ratcheted
up every nuance of fire and sensation.

When he stroked her, she pressed into his hand. Her soft
moan told him she liked what he was doing. Her hand reached
out and he realized she was unfastening the buttons on his
flannel shirt. When he anticipated her hands on him, he
thought he might spontaneously combust. If she was going
to feel *his* skin, then he was damn well going to feel *hers*.

Her hand slipped between the plackets of his shirt, and
his groan was gut-deep. His hand dropped from her breast,
passed down her side to lift her sweater. But when he did,
he felt the tautness of her stomach…and he froze. The

baby kicked under his hand. He remembered the night she'd asked if he wanted to feel, and he'd shut down.

She was carrying Alex's baby. Feeling the child inside her move, the reality of Alex's son or daughter became even more evident. This baby would bind Kylie to his brother for the rest of her life.

Soon she was going to have his brother's baby. And, in spite of what Alex had done to her, he knew she still loved him and would grieve for him for a long time. Brock had been second-best to Alex all of his life. He wouldn't be that now with him dead.

She must have known what he was thinking. She must have sensed his shock at feeling the baby move. She leaned away the same moment he did.

His eyes opened and so did hers. They stared at each other while they breathed in unison, gaining control over desire that had flared too quickly and still hadn't ebbed away.

"You felt the baby kick," she said softly.

"Yes, I did. Soon you'll look into your baby's face, see Alex and remember everything you loved about him. That's all that will matter."

He saw that she wanted to protest, yet couldn't, because what he'd said was the truth.

Crossing her hands over her belly, she stared straight ahead for a few moments. Then she gazed at him again. "You don't have to stay. I'm back to work now. Somehow, Dix and I will manage."

"Do you want me to go?"

"No, I don't, but for selfish reasons. I feel safe with you here. Like I don't have the burden of the world just on *my* shoulders."

"You and Dix can't handle this place over the winter. You know that. Besides the regular chores, when snow comes, Dix will have to lay out feed for the cattle. Not to mention the fact he'll have to cut more wood and make sure the horses are exercised."

When she laid her hand on his forearm, that desire he'd rounded up so expertly slipped out of the pen again.

She was still a bit flushed and her lips were pink from being kissed. "Let's call the real estate agent soon," she suggested. "Let's sell off those sections and get the capital I need so you can leave."

"Are you sure that's what you want to do?"

"It's the only solution. I should have done it before now. I was trying to keep Saddle Ridge intact. But that's not as important as getting it running again. With the money I can hire somebody part-time who can stay after the baby's born. I don't want to be an obligation to you, Brock. Not ever."

She was giving in to what he had decided was best after he'd returned. So why was he unsettled by the idea? It didn't matter. It was a solution.

Chapter Seven

"There it is," Garrett said, talking into his headset so Brock could hear him in spite of the Skyhawk's engine noise.

Saddle Ridge stretched out below, acres and acres and acres of it.

When Garrett had phoned Brock on Wednesday afternoon and asked if he wanted to drive out to the hangar to see the Skyhawk, Brock had accepted the offer, deciding he could use some male companionship his own age. Dix was great, but sometimes they seemed worlds apart.

After Brock had arrived at the hangar and looked over the plane, Garrett had asked if he wanted to go up.

Recognizing landmarks, the curves and twists of Mustang Creek, the stands of Russian olive trees and cottonwoods on the north sections, the windmill not far from a fence line weathered more than some of the others, Brock told Garrett, "Those are the sections she's planning to sell."

"Whoever buys that property will have a great view of the Painted Peaks."

Brock knew the property was prime real estate. He just hoped whoever developed it designed houses worthy of their surroundings. "You live in the foothills, don't you?"

"Sure do. You'll have to drive over sometime to see the place. Come spring, we're putting on that addition."

The two men were silent a few moments, taking in the purple and red hues of the mountains, the winter wheat, the sections employed for grazing cattle, others for sugar beets.

"Are you coming to my wedding?" Garrett asked. "You're invited."

"Thanks. Kylie mentioned Gwen said I could come along. Are you getting nervous?"

"Nah. Not this time. But it's Gwen that makes the difference, not the fact that I'm getting married again. I know this is right."

After a thoughtful moment, Brock asked, "You weren't sure the first time?"

"I'm not sure what I was the first time. Maybe I simply thought it was time to settle down. Maybe I was tired of sleeping alone. Whatever the case, I didn't really know Cheryl. How about you? Gwen mentioned you're divorced. Did you think it was right when you got married?"

"When I married Marta, the pieces seemed to fit. We were in the same line of work. I thought that mattered."

"It didn't?"

"Not in a crucial way. In fact, it masked the differences between us."

"I can see how that would happen. When you meet, when you're getting to know each other better, you'd have work to talk about. Other subjects might not come up."

"Exactly."

After both men spent the next few minutes examining the landscape, Garrett remarked, "I was years ahead of you in school. Did you play sports?"

"No. Jack, my father, believed working on Saddle Ridge was better than any sport." At least for Brock. While he had done chores, Alex had practiced roping calves or cutting cows. At least on weekends, Jack had let Brock work the horses, and that's what he'd liked to do best.

"This is a tough time for Kylie," Garrett commented. "But she's one strong lady."

"Too strong sometimes," Brock muttered.

Garrett cast him a quick glance. "I think Gwen and Shaye and Kylie have helped foster that quality in each other. They're tight. I didn't understand it when I first met Gwen, but now I do. I don't think men form that kind of bond."

"I have friends I know I can count on, but you're right. I think Gwen and Kylie and Shaye are more sisters than Alex and I were ever brothers."

"I don't have brothers or sisters. Gwen's the only person I ever felt an immediate connection with. That connection has grown stronger every day since."

Brock had always felt a connection with Kylie. "Are you going on a honeymoon?" Brock asked.

"Just a short one for now. We're flying to Las Vegas until the day after New Year's. Commercial flight," he added with a smile. "Gwen gets antsy when she's away from

Tiffany and Amy too long. She has Shaye on call in case Tiffany needs something."

"We're around, too," Brock offered, then wondered why it seemed so natural to say it.

"Thanks. Gwen will appreciate knowing that."

The Skyhawk was headed west now and Brock picked up the binoculars he'd brought along, putting them to his eyes.

"Looking for something in particular?"

"Teepee rings near the watering tank—the stones that held the covers of the teepees to the ground. Hunting parties would watch for buffalo, deer and elk."

"And these rings survived?"

"For the most part. In the winter you can usually see them. There," Brock said, pointing to almost indistinguishable rock circles.

As Garrett banked the plane and came around to fly over them once more, Brock was suddenly glad Kylie felt the way she did about Saddle Ridge. Another woman might sell the whole place to a developer without thinking twice. That shouldn't bother him, but it did. He liked the idea that those rings might be there for another hundred years. He'd always been viscerally pulled toward them. When Jack made him feel as if he were an outsider, Brock had ridden to them, as if they were a shrine to *his* heritage. And, maybe they were.

Right now they signified the circle he had to complete. When he'd left Saddle Ridge the first time, he'd been escaping, willing to make a life anywhere but here. This time, when he left, he'd do so without regrets.

That's why he had to stay away from Kylie.

He'd make sure Saddle Ridge was on the road to prosperity again, so he could leave in peace.

* * *

Kylie was sitting in the craft room at the table busily stitching a crocheted donkey's head to its body when Brock came home. She'd heard the truck on the gravel outside. She'd heard the front door open and close. She'd heard his boots on the steps. As soon as he stood in the doorway, watching her, she was aware of him there, too.

They'd stayed out of each other's way since they'd kissed, obviously uncomfortable with what had happened between them. She'd told herself she'd been susceptible to their attraction because she was insecure about her attractiveness, because Alex's betrayal had dented any confidence she had as a woman. Deep down, though, she knew none of that was true. Her feelings for Brock, even as a teenager, had gone deep and maybe now she was just realizing how deep.

She saw he'd brought the mail in from the end of the lane. "Anything important?"

"I don't think so. I just looked through it briefly while I was carrying it up." He nodded to the donkey in her hands. "If you get the kind of money I think you will for that land, you can buy Timmy and Amy anything you want for Christmas."

"I don't count my chickens before they're hatched," she quipped. "How did you like Garrett's plane?"

"I got the same feeling up in the plane that I get when I'm racing Rambo across the south pasture. The plane's older. It was his dad's. But he's kept it in great condition."

So she wouldn't forget what she was about—Brock had the habit of making her do that—she dipped the needle into the yarn one last time, knotted it and snipped it with her sewing scissors. Then she set the grey, fuzzy stuffed animal on the table.

Brock laid a stack of mail beside it. The corner of an oversized brown envelope shifted and she read the address. It was from the motel where Alex had stayed during his last rodeo.

"What's wrong?" Brock must have seen some change in her, and she felt the change in herself.

Her fingers were a bit quivery as she picked it up. "The return address. That's the motel in Las Vegas where Alex stayed. I spoke to the motel manager after Alex's accident. He sent all of his belongings here to me."

"You won't know what's in the envelope until you open it."

That was practical reasoning. She pinched the clip on the manila envelope, then slipped a finger under the flap to tear it open. Inside, she found a smaller manila envelope with a piece of hotel stationery clipped to it. The note read:

Dear Mrs. Warner,

A maid found the enclosed papers stuck in back of the desk drawer in the room your husband occupied. Obviously, our customers don't normally use the desks, or our maids don't clean very well, or this would have come to light sooner. All of us here at the Westward Ho send our condolences once more.

Sincerely,

Joe Conroy

"A maid found these in the back of the desk drawer in the room where Alex stayed," she explained.

Quickly now, she opened the flap of the second

envelope and reached inside. There wasn't much—a promotional brochure describing the rodeo Alex had participated in. It was a tri-fold flyer and inside the first flap were two other items. One was a receipt from Alex's entrance fee. The other was a plain white envelope. Opening it, Kylie expected to find ticket stubs or something like that. Instead, she found a piece of hotel stationery folded in half. Her name stared up at her from the first line…in Alex's handwriting.

"It's from Alex to me," she murmured, her voice a low whisper.

"A letter he never sent?"

"I guess. It only looks half-finished." She began to read.

Kylie,

Because I'm here for a week, I decided to write down some of my thoughts and send them to you. We aren't talking very well these days, and I guess that's my fault. We didn't leave anything in good shape before I left. I didn't get a goodbye kiss, and I didn't deserve one. There's so much I need to tell you and I can't do it over the phone. My words would get all jumbled up. You said if I didn't go to counseling with you, you'd leave. I can't even get my words out to *you*, let alone sitting in front of a third person. But I guess that's part of the process we might need. I know I didn't react well when you told me you were pregnant. Of course I shouldn't have blamed you. I was definitely there. When you told me you were going to have a baby, all I could see were more bills. More ties. More reasons I couldn't get away.

I can hear you now, darling, asking, "Alex, why do you want to get away?"

Maybe that's what I need a third person to tell me. I'm not sure why. I just know I can't abide the thought of you leaving. I want to change, darling. I really do. But I don't know how.

I do know the thought of a baby makes me want to run harder and faster than I've ever run. Me? A father? I wouldn't know what to do first. But maybe you can help me figure it out. Maybe someone else can help me figure it out. I've gotta go now, because Bumble Buck is calling. He's supposed to be the meanest and wildest of the bulls here. When I get back tonight, I'll finish this. Maybe I'll put down some of the things that will be hard to tell you face to face.

Tears were coursing down her cheeks and she hadn't even been aware of them. Now she looked up at Brock. "He never finished it."

"Do you mind if I read it?" Brock asked evenly.

Shaking her head, she handed it to him.

After Brock read it quickly he said, "You were going to get what you wanted. My guess is he would have confessed his affair and asked you to forgive him."

"Do you think he meant what he said?"

"There's no way to know. You've got it in black and white, so believe it if you want to."

She did desperately want to believe Alex's words.

Brock could obviously see that. "I'm going to check in with Dix."

As he left, she closed her eyes.

Could her life get any more confused than it was?

* * *

When Brock found Kylie in the baby's room the following evening, she was placing bibs in the drawer. They hadn't discussed Alex's letter last night. What was there to say? That letter would cause Kylie's grief to cut deeper, her loss to loom even bigger.

Brock was in turmoil about all of it himself. About his desire for Kylie that seemed rooted in the past, and a yearning that had no future. She'd been distracted last night and he'd left her alone.

"It looks as if you're ready," he said as an opener. The baby cradle had a mattress now and it was covered by a sheet in blue and pink stripes. A baby monitor sat on the chest and three packages of diapers were stacked near the changing area.

"The end of January is coming fast. I'd better be ready. I got one of those pay-as-you-go cell phones in town. I hung the number on the refrigerator."

He handed her a legal-sized envelope. "The man who bid on the mechanical bull came and got it. There's the six thousand dollars in a cashier's check."

"You keep it," she said quickly, not touching the envelope. "You bought the truck."

"You don't have to repay me for the truck." It was no surprise Kylie was going to be stubborn about this, but he could be stubborn, too. "This will hold you over for a little while until we get the land listed and sold."

"I don't want to be indebted to you."

"Why? If Alex had asked, I would have helped him out. You're no different."

When she looked ready to protest, he went on, "If I had needed a truck, would you have helped *me?*"

After a few moments of silence, she nodded. "Yes."

"Okay, then. The next time I need a truck I'll call you."

She gave him a smile, but it wasn't a real, Kylie smile. There was more effort behind it than genuine emotion. Finally taking the envelope, she looked at it for a while, then back at him. "I've been thinking about Alex's letter."

"I figured you might be."

"I want to believe he meant what he said in it."

"But?"

"But you knew Alex. He could say one thing today and do something different tomorrow. That night, maybe he really felt the sadness. Maybe he didn't want me to leave. But as far as changing… Do you believe people can change?"

"I think it's tough. I think they have to have motivation. Maybe you walking out or the baby being born would have given him motivation."

"Then there's Trish. What was he going to do about her?"

"You've got to stop beating yourself up over Alex's mistakes."

"Why did he start up with her, Brock? Why?"

He closed his hands on her shoulders and held her. "It was *not* your fault he slept with another woman. I honestly doubt that she was the first."

"Is that supposed to make me feel better?"

Swearing, he shook his head. "No. Of course it's not. But it shows you a pattern. You weren't the one who was lacking. Alex was. Can't you see that?"

"I can only see that my marriage didn't work. That something was wrong, maybe from the very beginning."

"Maybe he was the wrong man for you."

"Maybe I was the wrong woman for him." As Brock started to protest, she kept going. "Maybe he married me because I was safe. He knew I wouldn't demand too much. He knew I wouldn't make him give up his rodeoing. Maybe he even knew he could pull the wool over my eyes. What does that say about who I am?"

"It says that you expected him to be true to his word, just like you were true to yours. That's all it says, Kylie."

When she would have pulled away, he brought her close for a hug. Just a hug. He breathed in her scent, ran his hand down the back of her hair, felt desire fire up and want to run rampant. But he just held her, comforting her, knowing that was all he could do at this moment. All that she would accept. All that he should give. She had too many questions and no answers.

But maybe he could get a few of those answers for her. Maybe he could pay a visit to Trish Hammond to find out if she was everything Kylie thought she was. After all, monsters in the dark were always bigger than monsters chased down by the light of day. Maybe Trish Hammond wasn't as important as Kylie thought. Of course, the mistress wouldn't reveal that to the wife. But she might admit it to *him*.

When Kylie pulled away from him, her eyes were wet, and he just wished he could bring some joy and happiness into her life again. Christmas was only eleven days away. He was going to think of something special that would put a sparkle back into her eyes and bring a genuine smile to her lips.

"Thank you, Brock," she said, backing up a few steps. "If I have a little boy—"

"Don't say you're going to name him after me. This kid needs a fresh start. Pick a name no one in this family has ever seen before."

She laughed. "Shaye did give me a book of baby names. Maybe I'd better start looking through it if I expect the right one to just pop up after the baby's born."

"Speaking of, I don't want you to worry about what the hospital's going to cost. Your health and the baby's are more important."

"Actually, I was going to bypass that whole thing."

"Just how are you going to do that?"

"By using a midwife and having a home birth."

"You can't be serious!" Just the thought of Kylie in labor put him in a tailspin. She needed to be in a hospital with doctors who knew what they were doing.

"I'm not going to have a major argument with you about this. A home birth can even be better for the baby—without the bright lights, the noise, the loud voices."

"The doctors and nurses who know what they're doing—" Brock interjected.

"A midwife is trained and an obstetrician and a pediatrician are on call. It would be safe. I wouldn't do anything to put this baby in harm's way. You should know that."

"Kylie, you shouldn't let money dictate what you do."

"I'm not. Honestly, I'm not. I talked to my obstetrician about this. Wanda Lassiter, who's a certified midwife, is stopping by tomorrow. If you want, you can meet her."

"I want," he said tersely.

"You know, sometimes I think you're a throwback to a time when men believed women should just stay home and have babies."

"I respect professional women. I respect what you do with horses. But don't you want to stay home and have babies? Isn't that what you've always wanted?"

"Just like most women these days, I want to do work I like and be a mom, too. I just never thought I'd be doing it alone. Alone, I have to be as good as two parents. I have to be willing to do things maybe some women wouldn't."

"Such as?"

"Such as managing Saddle Ridge, choosing new stock, buying equipment, schooling and boarding horses, as well as feeding, diapering and rocking my baby."

"You can't do it all. No woman can."

"Never say 'can't' with me, Brock. It just makes me more determined to try." She crossed to the door. "I put a roast in the Crock-Pot this morning. We had potatoes left over from last night. After I steam a vegetable, supper will be ready."

"And heaven help me if I ask if you need help."

"If you'd like, I'll let you carve the roast."

He laughed and shook his head, then motioned to the stairs. "Lead the way." He knew Kylie talked a good game. She was a determined lady. But he also knew she needed someone to support her. For now, he was the one who was going to do it.

One way or another.

When Trish Hammond stepped into the office of Clementine's Friday evening, she was smiling. "Charlie said you wanted to talk to me. It's my break, so I have a few minutes. He said his son knew you back in high school. Charlie didn't tell me your name, though."

"It's Brock. Brock Warner."

At that, Trish's smile faded.

"I told him not to tell you my name. I wanted to make sure you'd talk to me."

Her hands went to her hips, to the short black skirt that ended midthigh over the black fishnets. "I only have a short break. What do you want?"

"Do you know who I am?"

"Yeah. You're Alex's brother. He mentioned you now and then."

If he was the curious type, he'd probe to find out exactly what Alex had said. But it didn't matter. "I hear you called Alex's wife."

"So what?" Her face was all defiance.

"I'd like to know why."

"What's it to you? She knows why."

"No, I'm not sure she does. She said you wanted to return Alex's belt buckle, but I don't think that's the real reason you called her to come here, is it?"

Trish's fingers fiddled with the shiny silver belt buckle at her waist. "Maybe it was, and maybe it wasn't. I don't see why you're concerned."

"You slept with a married man and you wanted to rub that fact into his wife's face. Are you just naturally vindictive or did you have a good reason for wanting to do that?"

Trish turned to go and Brock knew he'd made a mistake. He'd let his temper get the best of him. "Wait."

"Why should I, if you're just going to insult me?"

"That's not my intention. Kylie's going to have Alex's baby at the end of January. She was in an accident after her visit to you."

"I heard. That wasn't *my* fault."

"No, it wasn't. The truck broke down. Fortunately, she's recovered physically from her injuries. But emotionally, there's a lot going on *because* of her grief, because of her loss, because of *you*."

"Does she know you're here?"

"No. I'm not trying to create more stress for her. I'm trying to alleviate it. I think you wanted to meet Kylie and see what she was like. I think Alex probably told you about her, and maybe you were jealous. How am I doing?"

To his surprise, he saw tears well up in Trish Hammond's eyes. She cleared her throat. "I thought he was going to leave her and marry me. I thought I'd be the mistress of Saddle Ridge. I thought I'd go to all those rodeos with him and watch him win, and I could give up waitressing forever."

"Did Alex promise you all of that?"

"No, not in so many words. Finally, I knew why."

Brock just waited. He imagined Trish hadn't talked about this with many people, and it seemed whatever she had to say was aching to come out.

"He called me the night before he was killed." The tears welled up again and she blinked fast. "He told me he wasn't going to see me anymore. He told me when he came back here, we were finished."

"Did he tell you why?"

"He said Kylie was pregnant. He couldn't imagine being a father, but he was going to give it a damn good try. He said he was going to change his ways and be the kind of husband she deserved...if she stuck by him. Damn it, *I* wanted to be the wife he deserved. *I* wanted to be the one he came home to. I wasn't interested in having kids, but I wanted Alex. And he knew it."

"How long were you two involved?" Brock asked the question, although he'd had a pretty good idea because of the credit card statements he'd seen.

"About a year, maybe a little longer."

Brock's anger toward Alex was so immense he could hardly restrain it. His brother hadn't valued Kylie *or* his marriage. Yet, on the other hand, he'd decided to make it all right. That's all that would matter to Kylie now.

Trish looked down at the floor then back up at him. "Since July, I've tried to let it go. I've tried to let go of Alex. But the fact that he was going back to her just ate at me. I had to see her, meet her, find out why he couldn't give her up."

Brock asked, "Did you find out why?"

"She's nothing special. He was only going back to her because of the baby."

Brock wanted to shout his disagreement. Everything about Kylie was special.

"I gotta get back out there," Trish murmured.

"I know you do. Thanks for answering my questions."

She took another look at Brock, and then smiled. "Alex said you were a big time geologist and traveled all over the place. He looked up to you, you know. He said you had every reason to hate him, but you didn't. You just didn't come around anymore."

Brock's chest tightened. "He thought that was *his* fault?"

"He wasn't sure. He thought maybe you just couldn't stand to be in Wild Horse Junction any longer. Whatever it was, he was always glad when you called."

Guilt stabbed Brock again. He should have called more. He should have come back here more. He should have done a lot of things.

Before Trish left the office, she looked as if she were going to say something else, but then she shook her head. "Never mind. I was going to tell you you could buy me a drink some night when you came around. But you're not the type."

"Type?"

"Yeah. You're the *one*-woman type."

He didn't answer. Seconds later, she'd disappeared down the hall. The scent of Trish's perfume lingered in the office. It was way too strong.

When he told Kylie what Trish had said, she'd be tied to Alex even more tightly.

But he had to tell her. It was the right thing to do.

Kylie carried Brock's clean clothes from the laundry room beside the kitchen into his bedroom.

His bedroom.

It was ironic that it had once belonged to Jack. But only Brock's presence was evident now. The king-size, four-poster bed took up most of the room. A blue, yellow and red patchwork quilt Kylie had made draped over the sides onto the blue dust ruffle. There were blinds at the windows with red valances. A pair of Brock's jeans lay over a cane-seated chair, while his flannel shirt hung around the back. His work boots sat next to the dresser. That meant he'd changed into his good boots. After supper he'd said he had an errand to run. She hadn't asked where. It really was none of her business, but she was curious now. This time of year, shops and stores were open later, just as they were during the tourist season in the summer. Maybe he was buying his mother something for Christmas. She had just finished her own mom's beaded purse and would send it out on Monday.

Stopping at the bed, she separated his clothes into three piles—a jeans pile, a shirt pile and an underwear pile with both T-shirts and briefs. As she slid her hand over the more intimate clothing, her heart beat faster. She remembered his touch…his kiss…and why they'd broken apart.

She was so lost in the vivid images, she was startled when he said her name. Standing in the doorway to the bedroom, he was watching her.

Feeling flustered, knowing heat was flowing into her cheeks, she explained hurriedly, "I just brought your laundry in. I was separating it for you. Not that you need it separated, but I thought it might be easier—"

His strides were quiet, smooth, quick. Towering over her, he gave her a half smile. "I know you didn't come in here to steal my best pair of spurs."

Try as she might, she couldn't get the image of him in briefs out of her head. A few hot days when she'd worked beside him on the ranch, she'd seen him shirtless. She knew there was a smattering of black hair on his chest. The tufts of black hair against his bronze-hued skin had been mesmerizing. Back then, the tummy-twirling sensations she'd experienced had made her realize she was becoming a woman. Now, they seemed something forbidden. Something she shouldn't welcome. Something that could cause her more heartache.

Grabbing for any conversation she could think of that wouldn't land them into a mess of trouble, she asked, "Was downtown busy tonight?"

"As busy as Wild Horse gets. Lots of folks were Christmas shopping."

Curiosity got the better of her. "Is that what you were doing?"

"No."

She just waited, hoping he'd tell her.

"I went to Clementine's."

That declaration took her by surprise. "Was happy hour still going on?" she asked lightly.

"I didn't go there for happy hour. I went to see Trish Hammond."

Shocked, she blurted out, "Why?"

"Because you deserve to know the truth."

"And you think she'd tell you what that was?"

"I don't think she would have told *you*. I had to poke and prod a little, but I learned what I wanted to know."

Kylie started for the door. "I don't want to know any details. I don't want to know what she said about Alex. I don't want to know any of it."

Catching her, he held her fast. "Yes, I think you do. You might not want to know all of it, but I think you need to hear it."

"Why are you doing this?" she asked almost in a whisper. "How can I put everything behind me if we keep uprooting it? Nothing she had to say—"

"Listen to me, Kylie. Before he was killed, Alex called Trish. He told her they were finished. He wanted to put his marriage with you back together. That's why she was so vindictive. That's why she wanted to try to humiliate you. Because *she'd* felt humiliated. She thought she'd lost, and she wanted you to hurt more than you were already hurting."

There was pity in Brock's eyes and she couldn't bear that. She closed hers. Alex had really meant what he had written to her. There might be pity in Brock's eyes, but he'd given her a gift—a gift more valuable than any she'd ever received. Her husband had loved her, had been committed to her in his way. Whether they would have succeeded at putting their marriage back together again, she'd never know. But it renewed her faith in Alex that he'd wanted to try. It took some of the sting of betrayal away. Some.

"Don't disappear on me," Brock demanded.

Opening her eyes, she looked straight into his. "I'm not. I'm thinking how grateful I am that you've done this for me. It means more than I can ever tell you."

"Trish wasn't the kind of woman Alex ever would have married. *You're* the woman he wanted for his wife."

"Did you learn anything else?"

"I thought you didn't want to know details."

"I'm not sure I do. But I can't be a coward about it."

"I asked her how long it had been going on. She told me about a year."

"A whole year," Kylie murmured.

"It was just sex to him, Kylie. It had to be, or he couldn't have broken it off so easily."

"We don't know he did it easily. We don't know that at all. He gave her one of his belt buckles. They were important to him."

"They were trophies. But he had so many, he wouldn't miss one. Trish was just another adrenaline rush. You know Alex lived for them."

His fingers tightened on her shoulders. "I know what you're thinking. Don't. He kept coming back to you, Kylie. You grounded him. You were his home as much as this place."

How she wanted to believe that. How she wanted to

believe that she and Alex had had something genuine. Something real. At least at the beginning.

Standing on tiptoe, she kissed Brock's cheek.

"What was that for?" His voice was husky, as if her gesture of affection had affected him.

"For going out of your way to protect Alex's memory for me."

Bringing his hand to her cheek, he ran his thumb down the side of her face. "I guess I'm still trying to protect him, as well as you."

She wasn't sure what might have happened, then, with emotion running high between them…with the bed less than a foot away. But the phone rang.

She jumped. Brock picked up the receiver on the nightstand. "Saddle Ridge."

After listening for a few moments, he held it out to her. "It's Lily Reynolds."

Putting the receiver to her ear, she greeted the gallery owner, who was also becoming a friend. "Hi, Lily. What's up?" Where Brock's thumb had traced a line down her face, she could still feel the fire from his touch.

"I hope I'm not calling too late," Lily said. "I just closed the shop."

"No, it's not too late." She pictured Lily as she turned her attention to her, trying not to be distracted by Brock. Lily had Hopi blood in her background, and was exotically beautiful, with black hair and blue eyes. She'd returned to Wild Horse Junction a couple of years ago.

"I know with Christmas and all and you being pregnant your time is limited, but I sold the last purse of yours that I had in the case. The barrettes went yesterday to a customer who ordered from the Web site. So I'm calling to tell you that if you have any time at all, I'd love to have more of your creations."

"Soon, no one will be Christmas shopping."

"That doesn't matter. My Web clients are picking up and I could put whatever you give me on there, too. Dylan's photographs and prints have brought a lot more traffic to the store and to the Web site. So I'm selling more of everything. Don't do more than you can handle, but when you can't sleep at night, I'd like a few more beaded pieces."

Kylie laughed. "I'll get to work on something tonight or tomorrow. Do you want the same designs or different ones?"

"Whatever you can give me. Honestly, the beadwork you do is beautiful."

"All right. I'll see what I can do. I'll give you a call when I have something finished."

"Sounds good. Will you be coming into town for the First Night celebration?"

"I hope to. After all, I was on the committee that planned it. I don't want to miss the mustang racing through town to bring in the New Year. I just wish I could ride him."

"Next year," Lily suggested.

"We'll see. I'm taking one day at a time."

"I'll look forward to seeing you. Make sure you stop in and say hi before or after work some day."

"I'll do that. Thanks again, Lily."

"No. Thank you. I'll send you your check."

After Kylie put the phone back on the nightstand, Brock guessed, "She wants more of your work."

"Yes. Isn't that great?"

"You can add it to the nest egg for your baby."

"Yes, I can."

"I hear you when you work at your table at night. The floor creaks when you move the chair. Some nights you don't turn in until three o'clock."

"The baby kicks most around midnight. It's crazy. Or maybe I'm just more aware of it because I'm trying to go to sleep. But if I work for a while, he or she settles down."

"You need your sleep."

"Tell that to my ballerina or soccer player."

"Which do you really want?"

"I have to admit, I'd love a little girl, so I could share girlie things with her. Not only that, I worry about having a boy, since he won't have a role model."

"I think he'd have role models. You'd probably make sure he'd form close ties with Dylan and Garrett."

"I guess that's true. You know, *you* could be an important influence in his life, too, if you wanted to be. If you came back here to visit. The way to erase bad memories is to make new ones. You could do that with this child."

One look at Brock's face told her just the thought stirred up turbulent emotions. He'd be a wonderful role model. He'd be an even better dad.

She could picture him as this baby's father. Even more than she could ever picture Alex being a father. She suddenly realized she wished Brock *were* the father…this baby's real dad.

Aware she was in Brock's bedroom, aware her feelings for him were growing deeper, aware that she couldn't carry regret and guilt and "what-ifs" and "if-onlys" for the rest of her life, she hoped Brock would give her an indication of what he was thinking.

But he didn't. He simply nodded. "That's something to consider. Now how about a cup of that sleepy-time tea. Maybe it will put the baby to sleep, too."

"You're going to drink tea?"

"I didn't say that. I'll brew a pot of decaf. Then neither of us will be wandering around the house tonight."

Did Brock have insomnia, too? Or did he think about her in bed, the same way she thought about him in bed?

She wouldn't ask that question because it was better for her right now if she didn't know the answer. She had to stay focused on her baby and Saddle Ridge. Then maybe the rest of it would fall into place.

Chapter Eight

In the barn, Kylie felt peaceful. In the barn, she could escape the constant tugging toward Brock that kept her awake at night and restless during the day. In the barn, she could remember being a kid playing with kittens in the hay bales, riding bareback through the fields, letting whatever cares she had blow away like leaves in the wind. She couldn't do much here this late in her pregnancy, but she loved the smells of old wood, clean hay and saddle leather that had seen years of use.

She was cleaning tack after work on Monday when Dix came into the barn. He frowned at her. "You should be up at the house. It's too cold and damp for you to be out here."

"Don't start, Dix. I can't stay cooped up in the house until this baby's born. We both need fresh air and a change of scene."

"Brock said you're not sleeping at night."

"What do you two do, give each other daily reports on my health?"

"Now don't go getting in a snit because we want to look after you."

With a sigh, she set aside the jar of leather cleaner and the rag. "Did you come out here to lecture me, or is there something that needs my attention?"

She was still trying to work through Alex's letter and the fact that Brock had taken it upon himself to confront Trish Hammond. Had he simply wanted to put her mind to rest? Or had he wanted to prove to himself that his brother was a scoundrel rather than just a complicated cowboy who hadn't known what he really wanted in life? So much went on under the surface with Brock. So much, that maybe he, himself, wasn't even aware of it.

"There isn't anything going on that Brock and I can't take care of," Dix reassured her, as if that *were* reassuring. "But I thought you might want to know he's back from town. I saw him carrying something inside that looked like it belonged in the nursery."

When Brock had told her he was going into town to an electronics store to buy a GPS unit to plot coordinates on the ranch, she hadn't thought much of it. She'd just told him they'd have a late supper. "I don't need anything else for the nursery. What was he taking inside?"

"If he meant it to be a surprise, I don't want to spoil it. Maybe you should go look."

Screwing the lid onto the leather cleaner, she set the jar on the shelf. "I am finished here for now. Did you see how well Feather is socializing with the other horses?"

"She seems to be fitting right in. Brock's doing a good job with her. He's almost as good as you are reading those critters' minds. Sometimes I wonder what would have happened if he would have stayed on and helped you and Alex make a go of this place. I bet everything would be different. He's got a knack for managing, a good eye for efficiency, not just with horses, but with the machines and the land. But I guess he became a geologist because he didn't want to stay in one place."

Kylie wasn't so sure of that. Brock had become a geologist because he *was* in tune with the land. Whether he'd admit it or not, Saddle Ridge meant something to him. Sure, there were bad memories here of times when Jack had pushed him aside and had used him as a hired hand, rather than treating him like a son. But Brock had walked these fence lines, not because he'd had to, but because he'd wanted to. He'd gentled and schooled horses because he'd had a talent for it, just as she had. He'd smelled the spring grass, gotten swallowed up in the huge sky and climbed the snow-capped Painted Peaks. Saddle Ridge and Wild Horse Junction were in his blood, whether he wanted to admit it or not. She couldn't discuss any of that with Dix, though. It seemed a betrayal of Brock somehow.

"Life for all of us would be very different if Brock had stayed. But he left and he's going to leave again."

"Once your baby's born, it might be harder for him to leave."

Or easier, she thought. Whenever he looked at Alex's child, he'd remember she was once his brother's wife. Alex would always be between them.

"I'll go to the house and take a peek at the nursery. But if you're pulling my leg just to get me out of here…"

"I'd never tell you a fib," Dix muttered with a smile.

"Mmm," was her noncommittal reply. "Why don't you come for supper with us tonight? I made shepherd's pie. I've been waiting for Brock to come home to put it in the oven."

"I don't want to intrude."

"I wouldn't ask you to join us if I thought you'd be intruding. You're family, Dix. Don't you know that yet?"

After he studied her for a few moments, he nodded. "Okay. Sounds better than warmed up corned beef hash."

A few minutes later, as Kylie let herself into the house, she wondered what Brock could have put in the nursery. The sound of water running in the downstairs bathroom told her he was probably washing up. Crossing to the refrigerator, she removed the casserole and slipped it into the oven. She took a whiff of the cinnamon bread she'd made that morning, loving the scent of cinnamon in the house, especially at Christmastime.

After Kylie climbed the stairs, she took the few steps to the nursery's doorway. There she stopped. A huge lump formed in her throat. Over by the crib stood a wooden clothes horse with a yarn mane. On its back sat a butterscotch-colored teddy bear. Walking over to the horse, Kylie picked up the bear. Its fur was as soft as a kitten's fur. She hugged it to herself as tears formed in her eyes. What had made Brock do this? Had he simply passed it in the window and decided to buy it for her baby? Had he gone looking for something special? Christmas was only a week away. He could have saved it until then.

Whatever the reason he'd bought it, she had to thank him.

Returning downstairs, she wasn't thinking of anything except giving him a hug when she headed for his room. The door was partially open and she went straight inside.

When she saw Brock, she froze and stared. He was stark naked with not even a towel slung around him. He was turned toward the dresser, pulling out a drawer. She must have made a sound because he swivelled around and she got a full frontal view. She knew she should turn and leave. She knew she should at least close her eyes. But a deep, womanly curiosity kept her rooted to the spot. Kept her looking. Kept her admiring. Kept her marveling at the sheer male beauty of him.

Somehow, her eyes finally drifted up to his. The collision shook her. She liked looking at him and she could see in the depth of his gaze, *he* liked her looking at him. Primal knowledge, attraction and anticipation thrummed between them until she realized exactly what was happening. They were both getting aroused. The state of *her* body was hidden. His wasn't.

Red-faced, she spun around and practically ran from his room.

"Kylie, wait."

Wait? Wait to see what would happen next? She didn't think so.

When she reached the living room, she stopped. What was she going to do? Run up to her bedroom and lock the door? That would do a lot of good.

Moments later, he was in the living room with her, clasping her arm. He was wearing jeans now, though they weren't snapped. All that tan, male flesh drew her eyes. She wanted to run her fingers through his chest hair.

"It's all right, Kylie. We're living under the same roof. Things like that are bound to happen."

Speechless with feelings that confused her and made her life even more chaotic, she just shook her head. "What's happening, Brock?"

Denial stole the concerned expression from his face. "Nothing's happening, Kylie."

What he meant was nothing emotionally was happening for him. What he meant was he was feeling pure, sexual attraction. And how was that possible with her in the last stages of her pregnancy? Whether he would admit it or not, they were connected again. On many levels. The problem was most of that connection was due to Alex.

Composing herself, knowing her pride was all she had to protect her, she decided, "The next time I come to your room, I'll definitely knock first."

"That might be safer," he agreed neutrally, releasing her arm.

She couldn't simply act as if she hadn't seen what she'd seen, as if a live current hadn't zipped between them. The image of him naked was branded before her eyes, and it would be a long time until it passed. However, she *could* go on as he was, pretending nothing had happened. "I came in to thank you for the clothes horse and the bear. That was thoughtful."

"Not a lot of thought behind it," he said offhandedly. "I got it at that little furniture store next to the hardware store. Wes Guloff makes all the furniture himself. He's got some wonderful pieces in there. I just thought it might come in handy. As the baby gets older, you can teach him how to hang up his clothes so they're not all over the floor."

"Or her," she returned, wondering if he was thinking about a boy who could run Saddle Ridge one day. A girl could do it, too, and Kylie was going to prove it.

"Now don't go all feminist on me. You know I'm a man who believes in equal opportunity for all."

That brought a smile to her lips. "You got out of that one nicely, didn't you?"

He seemed to relax a little more now that they were conversing about something that wasn't so personal. Now that they weren't simply reacting to each other.

"I'm going to finish getting dressed. These floors are cold," he joked.

Even when she looked down at his bare feet, she got a tingle from that. She had to do something about these reactions to him that were becoming harder to hide. "Tonight after supper I'm going to work on a beaded piece for Lily, so I'll be upstairs all night."

His knowing eyes told her he knew exactly what she was doing. But he didn't protest. "I have work-related calls to make and a prospectus to put together for investors, so I'll be down here. I won't bother you."

Brock simply being down here *would* bother her. But once she started the beadwork, she'd concentrate on that and nothing else.

She hoped.

A light snow began falling on December twenty-third as Brock drove Dix's pickup along the rutted path that was hardly a path any longer. He'd been using the GPS unit most of the day, attempting to forget about Kylie coming into his room several days ago. Every time their gazes met now, they had another lasting memory between them. Those memories were pushing them apart. Wasn't that the best thing that could happen?

What's happening between us, Brock? Kylie had asked, as if she'd really expected him to answer.

Long ago memories...imaginings of a man who should know better...the desires of a man who had been without sex for too long were what was happening. She'd have been hurt if he'd said that to her. Or maybe not. Kylie was tough. Tough on the outside, anyway. He doubted if she was any different on the inside. And that, damn it, was why he responded to her.

Although he was wearing his seat belt, Brock came off the seat as he ran over a rut and the truck jostled him. Straying away from the old vehicle path, he headed toward a gully, slowed, took the truck down the slope through the shallow water and up the other side. The grey sky was getting greyer by the minute and dusk would come early tonight. But he knew his way around this ranch as if it were the palm of his hand. He'd explored every inch of it as a kid. He knew exactly where he could see antelope run. He could predict whether the stream had gone dry or was still swelling, no matter what time of the year. He sensed where cattle had wandered to graze. A message in his soul had drawn him to the teepee rings over and over again. That's where he was headed now.

Before Jack had let him drive the vehicles on the ranch, Brock had walked out here. Hiked out here. Ridden horseback out here. Gotten lost out here. But lost was a state of mind, and he'd soon learned to memorize every stand of trees, the location of each windmill, the crests of hills and the dips into the valleys. Most of all, these rings. When life had gotten tough, he'd come out here, think about his mother on the reservation, make his own plans to leave and never come back.

The snow melted on the hood of his pickup, but he knew that could change as night fell and the temperature dropped. Since the other day, Kylie had been giving him unspoken messages. Stay out. Go away. Let me be alone with thoughts of my husband and my baby so I can sort it all out. He wondered if she'd ever sort it out. Since he'd told her about Trish, he wondered if she thought kindly of Alex again. Since she'd read his letter, had she forgiven her husband for everything he'd put her through? Was a woman's love so strong she could bear hurts and forgive them? Had Kylie's love been that strong?

Maybe that was the difference between men and women. A wife's unfaithfulness would stab so deep, Brock knew he could never trust her again. How could a marriage survive with a lack of trust? His hadn't. That had been a different kind of trust issue. They'd been so different. Marta had wanted a child so badly. But when she couldn't get pregnant, almost every look at him was one of resentment. He'd resented her, too, for basing marriage on the whim of fate bestowing a child...or not.

When he stepped on the brake, the truck lurched on the uneven ground. He got out, adjusted his hat and slammed the door. The teepee rings had looked much different from the plane with Garrett. He'd easily imagined the shelters rising up toward the sky, the hunting bands who had searched for food, the gatherings around the fires that had given hunters community. Now as he crouched down to touch a pile of rocks, they were slick under his fingers. As he followed the circle, he spotted another circle, and then another.

Life was made up of circles, he supposed. Some a man completed and some a man didn't. He was uncomfortable with the fact that his life had circled back here to Saddle Ridge...to Kylie. He should leave now, before the situation got even more complicated. Yet how could he leave with her baby due? How could he leave with the ranch still needing capital? How could he leave when he knew Kylie and Dix could never handle on their own the amount of work that was going to come?

You want to see Alex's baby, a whisper inside his head scolded.

No, he didn't. He did *not* want to see Alex's baby. He did not want to see a gift that fate had bestowed on his brother when he hadn't deserved it. Brock shook his head. He shouldn't judge. Maybe not fate but a Creator had decided this gift could turn Alex around.

Then why had he died?

Free will and all that. Religion had too many questions and not enough answers.

Looking up at the sky, letting the snow fall on his face, holding his arms wide, he felt the spirituality of the place—the life energy of a primitive people...people that hung onto old ways because new ones just didn't suit. All of his life he'd been able to find answers out here. He'd been able to find peace in the sun, and the snow, and the clouds and a Creator who looked down on him gently, expecting nothing in return—except to accept the acknowledgment of the goodness in his heart.

His heart had brought him back here when Kylie needed him. But now, his heart was looking for the easy road when there was none.

Because Alex was an obstacle on any road…an obstacle that couldn't be avoided.

"We're giving her that puppy that Seth took in," Amanda Daily confided to Kylie in a hushed voice as Molly went to the kitchen for napkins.

It was Christmas Eve morning, and Molly and her mom had stopped in for a visit. Kylie had made hot chocolate and opened a can of Christmas cookies.

Molly's mother was a pretty, auburn-haired woman, a few years older than Kylie.

"She'll love that a lot," Kylie replied. "Molly has seemed…quiet lately. Is she that way at home?"

Kylie had wanted to open a dialogue about what was troubling Molly, or at least give her parents a heads-up that something was. With Molly in the kitchen all she could do was drop a hint.

A shadow seemed to pass over Amanda's face. "Her father and I are trying to make a decision on what's best for her future. We don't agree and I think she feels that tension."

Her future? Kylie wanted to ask questions. Were they thinking of sending her to a boarding school? Or were they talking about college this early? Molly came back into the living room then with the napkins, and she couldn't pursue it. At least the Dailys were aware something was troubling their daughter. Kylie just hoped they could resolve it soon.

"I want you to open your present now." Molly was all smiles and enthusiasm and Kylie loved to see her that way.

Kylie was about to unwrap the box on her lap when the front door opened and Brock came in.

When he saw them all, he said, "Just passing through. I need a printout from upstairs."

"Have some hot chocolate with us," Molly invited him.

He looked as if he wanted to refuse, but then he nodded. "Okay. I can take a break for a few minutes."

"I'll make it for you just as soon as Kylie opens my Christmas present."

"I can make it myself," he said with a chuckle. But he didn't move. He was watching Kylie with the present.

With his gaze on her, Kylie's fingers weren't quite steady as she untied the bow and then unwrapped the box. Lifting the lid, she pushed back the tissue paper and found a small framed needlework plaque that read Cowgirl Up and had the outline of a horse. "It's terrific, Molly! I love it."

"I did it myself. I mean, the cross-stitch. Mom helped with the framing. You can put it in the barn, or anywhere you want."

"I'll have to think about it, but it might go upstairs in my bedroom."

Picking up the small box from the table beside her, Kylie handed it to Molly. "Your turn."

After Molly tore off the ribbon and paper she found two beaded barrettes inside. "They're gorgeous. Did you make these?"

"Sure did." Kylie had always believed there was something important about giving handmade presents. They seemed to carry so much more love with them. The socks she'd started for Brock were finished now. And wrapped. She hoped he understood how much…love they carried with them.

Love. She was in love with Brock Warner and there was nothing she could do about that.

"Are you okay, Kylie?" Amanda asked. "You look a little pale."

No, she wasn't okay. She was in love with Alex's brother, but there was a world of years and resentment between them. And he'd be leaving. He'd be going back to a life she knew nothing about.

She'd never expected he'd stay. But if he could exorcize his ghosts, couldn't he be happy on Saddle Ridge?

Even if he could, he'd never forget she was once married to his brother. He'd never forget she was having Alex's child.

"I'm fine. Just a little indigestion. It must have been the chocolate."

Brock came over beside her chair and looked at the plaque. "You did a great job with that, Molly."

"Thanks," she said, giving him a bright smile. An adoring, I-think-you're-master-of-the-world smile. Kylie knew the feeling.

After Brock made hot chocolate, he joined them for a few minutes, engaging in small talk and answering Molly's questions about Feather.

When there was a lull in the conversation, Molly said to Kylie, "Uncle Seth asked about you. He told me to wish you a very merry Christmas, and said maybe he'd see you at the First Night celebration. You are going, aren't you?"

"I wouldn't miss it," Kylie assured her. "But is your mom going to let you stay up that late?"

"We'll let her watch the mustang run through town.

Then we'll put her to bed." She checked her watch. "Honey, we really have to go."

"We're having a party tonight and we have to get ready," Molly explained, looking happy about it.

Kylie was glad to see that the ten-year-old's mood had lightened considerably, and she seemed almost her normal self. Christmas could do that.

Ten minutes later, Molly and her mom were leaving and Kylie was standing on the porch waving to them as they drove out the lane.

Brock slid his hands into his back pockets and stared into the distance away from the barn up into the Painted Peaks. "Maybe tonight I'll drop you off at Shaye's and then pick you up after the church service."

Kylie had explained to Brock she always spent Christmas Eve with Gwen and Shaye. They had, of course, also invited him to a party at Shaye's and then they'd all attend the midnight service at church.

"I thought you were going to go along with me."

"I never said that."

She sighed. "No, I guess you didn't. I should have guessed you…wouldn't want to go."

He frowned, looking miffed at her tone. "You're going to a party with your friends, Kylie. You said you've spent every Christmas Eve with them since you were a kid. Why would I want to barge into that?"

"Maybe because *you* are my friend, too? Maybe because Dylan and Garrett haven't been with us all those years, but they're part of our circle now."

"I'm not part of your circle."

"You could be," she said plainly. And boldly. She wasn't

sure what she was doing, but her realization that she loved Brock Warner was roiling inside of her until she had to let something out.

Instead of rebutting her claim, he simply asked, "What are you trying to do, Kylie?"

A shiver ran through her, more from the seriousness of their conversation than the cold. "I'm not trying to *do* anything, except maybe make Christmas a little easier for both of us."

"Do you think me spending time with your friends will make it easier?"

"I think friendship is one of the gifts I appreciate most at Christmas. Why can't you open your life and your heart a little so you're not walling everyone out?"

"When did this become about me?" he asked brusquely. "*You* want to go to a party. *You* want to go to church services. Fine. I'll be your chauffeur."

Abruptly she turned away from him and said over her shoulder, "I don't need a chauffeur. I'm quite capable of driving myself. Stay home and brood if you want, Brock. But on Christmas Eve, I'm going to be with the people I love."

As she stalked into the house, she heard him swear. But he didn't come after her. She was halfway through the living room when she realized the door was still hanging open and Brock had headed for the barn.

She felt like crying.

But she wasn't going to let even a few tears fall. She had Christmas presents to wrap and her famous chili dip to make to take along to the party. Just because her heart hurt, just because she had feelings for Brock that could never go anywhere, didn't mean she couldn't rise above all of it.

Her hand on her stomach, she felt her baby move. This baby was what Christmas was all about.

As Brock mucked out Feather's stall, he knew he'd handled everything about that encounter with Kylie badly. Every encounter with her lately seemed to end with acid burning in his stomach. Or his chest tight. Or his body revved up beyond rationality. There was no way he was letting her drive into town alone tonight. No way at all.

When Dix came into the barn, he asked, "Anything else you want me to do before I leave?"

Dix was driving to Cody to spend Christmas Eve with some relatives and staying overnight.

"No, we're caught up here. If you want to take off, go ahead."

"I have something to give Kylie first. Is she napping or anything?"

Brock practically guffawed. "Napping? I doubt that."

"Did you two have another go-around?" Dix asked perceptively.

Brock stopped shoveling. "She sure as hell has a mind of her own."

Although he tried hard, Dix couldn't suppress his grin. "That's news?"

Brock pushed his hat back farther on his head with the handle of the shovel, then propped it beside him. "I suppose not. But she sure digs in her heels when she gets an idea in her head."

"When Alex was alive, if she hadn't dug in her heels, they'd have lost this place altogether."

"After she sells a few sections, she'll be fine," Brock offered.

"Do you think so?" Dix asked, as if he didn't.

"Sure. Alex's baby will give her the motivation to make this place as good as it once was."

"That's the way you think of this baby she's carrying? As Alex's child?"

"That's what it is."

"This is *Kylie's* baby. The last time Alex left, he didn't want any part of it. Kylie will always remember that."

"He wrote her a letter before he died. He was going to try to make things right. She just got it in a package of stuff from the motel."

"I don't think one letter could make everything that was wrong between them right. Do you?"

"I don't know. That depends on how well Kylie can believe everything would have turned out for the best if he'd have come home."

In the silence, Brock heard the twist and squeal of the weathervane on the barn being blown by the wind. Taking the shovel in hand once more, he started back to work. "Do you mind if I ask what you got her for Christmas?"

"I don't mind. But I didn't buy her anything. I braided a halter for Feather. With my fingers getting stiff, it took a while. But it turned out okay."

Brock had always admired Dix's work. But with the outdoor chores, the cold and his age, his fingers weren't as nimble as they once were. Brock was sure that hadn't affected the quality of his work any. "I'm sure she'll like it."

"What are you getting her for Christmas?" Dix asked, wanting to know.

"Fifty head of prime Angus to be delivered in the spring, a new coat and that surprise in the tractor shed."

"You think she's going to accept fifty head of Angus?"

"She'll accept them. She might be stubborn, but she'd never hurt my feelings by not accepting my gift."

Dix chuckled. "You're smart, boy, I'll give you that. You have a good Christmas. I'll be back tomorrow evening."

If Brock was *smart,* he wouldn't be here now. If he was *smart,* he'd leave—sooner rather than later. But smart somehow got trampled by regrets and duty and a need he still didn't understand to be here right now.

An hour later, after Brock had heard Dix's truck rumble out the lane, he returned to the house. Kylie stood at the kitchen table, rolls of wrapping paper and spools of ribbon stacked on one chair. She was carefully folding what looked like a shawl and arranging it in a tissue-lined box.

"Did you make that?" he asked, more to make conversation than anything else.

"Yes. It's for Gwen. She loves shawls."

"That doesn't look knitted," he noticed.

"No, it's crocheted." The yarn was multicolored green and the wrap almost looked lacelike.

"Did you make Shaye's present, too?"

"I did. It's a leather purse with a beaded fringe."

"Are you going to exchange gifts tonight?"

"Yes, we are. I could just add your name to mine on the presents. Or are you still determined to spend Christmas Eve alone?"

Did he want to spend Christmas Eve alone? Or was he willing to jump into this circle of Kylie's, even if only for a short time?

Chapter Nine

"Great place you've got here," Brock told Dylan on Christmas Eve.

Brock had escaped the merriment of the Christmas party in the living room for a few minutes, but when he'd gotten to the kitchen, he'd found Dylan deep in the recesses of the refrigerator. He supposed being here tonight with Kylie's friends was better than sitting at Saddle Ridge rehashing the fact that last year he'd gone skiing to avoid the holidays after he and Marta had split up.

Emerging from the refrigerator with a baby bottle, Dylan straightened. "We like it. Timmy will have room to roam, and we have an extra bedroom for more kids."

"Did you build this?"

"Oh, no," Dylan replied with a shake of his head. "We decided to buy a house right after we got married. Building would have taken too long. This had been constructed as someone's vacation home, but the couple only kept it for two years and decided to sell because of the way real estate had boomed in the area. Kylie said she's planning on selling off some acreage. She could get good money for it."

"That's what we're hoping."

"We're glad you decided to come tonight." Dylan ran hot water over the baby bottle.

"Kylie twisted my arm," Brock replied truthfully.

Dylan laughed. "She can do that by raising an eyebrow, can't she?"

"Yep, she sure can."

"Are you going to be her coach for the baby?"

"No," was the answer that erupted from Brock's mouth, as if that was the most preposterous notion in the whole world. "Whatever gave you that idea?"

"Gwen mentioned Kylie was going to have a home birth. I thought since you were there…"

"Isn't that why the midwife is going to be there?" He still wasn't happy with the whole idea of a home birth.

"She'll be attending to Kylie and the baby. And she probably will coach if nobody else does."

"I don't know a thing about babies. Or about pregnant women," Brock added wryly.

Dylan chuckled. "I imagine one is as complicated as the other. Kylie might ask Gwen to coach since babies are her business." After a pause, he added, "Once I made up my mind to do it, I learned about babies really fast."

When Brock considered the reality that Dylan would be raising his sister's son, he wondered if Dylan felt like a real dad. He surely acted like one.

As if Dylan had read Brock's thoughts, he confided, "I can't wait until the adoption is final. It took me a few months to come to grips with wanting to be a dad, but after I did, there was no turning back. I can't imagine my life without Timmy."

"If you and Shaye have kids of your own, do you think it will be different?"

"You mean what I feel?" He shook his head. "Nope. Timmy's my son, and Shaye's…in every sense of the word. Along with him come all the memories of my sister and her husband. If anything, I feel even more bonded to him, more protective of him because of that."

"Kylie will remember Alex that way every time she looks at her baby." That was a fact Brock couldn't escape.

Turning off the water spigot, Dylan faced Brock. "I'm not sure that's the same thing at all."

"What do you mean?"

Looking conflicted, Dylan shook his head. "Alex was your brother. I shouldn't say anything."

"He was my brother, but my eyes were wide open where he was concerned."

Still Dylan didn't plunge into what he'd been thinking. "My memories of Julia and Will are all good ones. But Kylie and Alex—"

"Kylie stayed with my brother because she loved him."

"Yes, she did," Dylan responded. "But when I returned to Wild Horse, there was a sadness in Kylie. There still is now because she's grieving. Back then, disappointment was mixed in. I remember there had been an article in the paper about Alex winning a rodeo purse. He hadn't even told her about it. I mean, he was still out of town, I guess, but he hadn't even called her. If I'd won something like that, I'd be on the phone to Shaye the next minute. So I guess what I'm saying is that Kylie's probably carrying around a mixed bag of emotions where her marriage is concerned. When her baby's born, I don't think she's going to want to dwell on that. She's not that type of woman. She's going to get on with her life."

"You sound as if you know her pretty well." Brock found himself a mite resentful of that.

"With Kylie and Shaye being best friends, along with Gwen, their friendship spilled over on me. Oh, they keep their secrets, but I almost feel kind of brotherly toward Kylie. Do you know what I mean?"

"I guess I do."

"Even with Gwen." Dylan shook his head. "If it hadn't been for her, I might not have realized I wanted to marry Shaye for *my* sake as well as Timmy's. She read me the riot act one day like a sister would."

"You didn't have a problem with her poking into your private business?"

"That's just it, Brock. It wasn't exactly private. Those three women have a bond the likes that I've rarely seen. They're as protective of each other as *we* might be of them, so Gwen felt it was her business. I think of the three of them now, Kylie keeps the most to herself. But I'll never forget the first day I *really* talked to her. It was at Timmy's christening. She wasn't judging me or what I was trying to do, and that meant a lot."

"What you were trying to do?"

"Shaye was Timmy's legal guardian, due to my sister's will. When I decided I wanted to be his dad, Shaye's family resented me complicating her life. Understandably, they didn't want me to take Timmy away from her."

"Sounds sticky," Brock muttered.

"It was. But hard times sometimes cement relationships the way nothing else can."

Did Brock feel a bond with Kylie because they knew each other's history? Because they were part of each other's history?

A crying baby's wail sailed into the kitchen from the living room. "I think he's tired of waiting." Dylan dried off the bottle with a towel then crossed the room.

At the doorway he turned. "You might want to think about becoming Kylie's coach. I hear watching a baby come into the world is an awesome experience."

Then Dylan was gone and Brock was left with his troubled thoughts.

"May peace fill our hearts as we lift our voices in song."

The minister blessed the congregation and everyone opened their hymnals for the last hymn of the midnight service.

Next to Kylie, Brock heard the feeling she put into every word as her sweet voice floated high above his. He joined in. After all, it was Christmas Eve. Didn't everyone want to feel their hearts swell a bit on this night?

Instead of swelling, however, Brock's heart hurt. When he saw the tears rolling down Kylie's cheeks, it hurt even more. For her. For him. For Alex. For this baby.

More than anything, he wanted to put his arm around her, bring her close to him, let her know he was there. But he had no right to do that. He certainly didn't want to start gossip that she'd have to live with after he was gone. So he stood stoically beside her, letting his arm brush hers, as if that could give some small measure of comfort.

She glanced at him.

Their gazes met, and Brock felt the earth shift just a little bit more.

The church was an old one, built in the late 1800s. But the pews were shiny, as if someone had just polished them yesterday. As the churchgoers finished their songs, closed their hymnals and filed out of the pews, Brock took a long, last look at the poinsettias decorating the front of the church...the nativity scene in the corner...the baby in the manger.

Once they stood in the vestibule, he noticed Dylan hooked his arm around his wife, while Shaye stood rocking Timmy, who was asleep. Gwen, Garrett and Tiffany gave hugs all around, and Brock found himself included in their warm friendliness. Since Kylie had gotten hot during the service, she'd shed her coat. Now it hung loosely over her shoulders and, as someone brushed past them, it fell to the floor.

Brock stooped to pick it up. Holding it for her, he was aware of how pretty she looked tonight in her plaid dress. The peachy scent of her shampoo or lotion or whatever she wore was one he couldn't get out of his senses, even when he wasn't around her. It was homey and erotic at the same time, and it suited her perfectly. He just wished the scent didn't carry with it the powerful memories of their kiss.

As he held her coat for her, she slipped one arm into it. "Thank you," she murmured. When she caught the other arm, he noticed a gold chain around her neck. It wasn't very heavy and whatever dangled from it was hidden under her dress. It was hard for him to let go of the coat and not put his arms around her.

The moment was abruptly broken by Seth Buchanan, who came up to Kylie and did exactly what Brock had been thinking about doing. Only Seth was free and easy about the whole thing.

As he hugged Kylie and kissed her on the cheek, he said, "Glad to see you could make it. I thought maybe you'd be sticking close to home."

Not at all thrown by Seth's sign of affection, Kylie hugged him back. "I have a month or so. My due date's January twenty-ninth, but with the first baby, I understand anything could happen."

"Are you ready for it to be over?"

Wrinkling her nose, she considered his question. "In a way I am. But in another way, this time is precious. I can't wait to meet him or her, but I'll never go through a first pregnancy again, either."

A first pregnancy, Brock thought. Did that mean she was thinking about a second one? With someone like Seth? Maybe even *with* Seth?

"You'll forget about a first pregnancy with all the other firsts."

"That's what I'm afraid of, so I've been keeping a journal."

She had given Seth that information so easily, yet she had never told Brock she was keeping a journal.

When Brock took a proprietary step closer to her, Seth acknowledged him. "Hi, Brock. Good to see you again. I hear you're looking for a real estate agent."

Wild Horse Junction might have gotten a little bigger. Chain stores might be moving in. But the essential gossipy smallness of the town hadn't changed. "I've spoken to a couple of people. Haven't made a decision yet, though."

Kylie's eyebrows arched and her gaze asked why he hadn't told her.

"I'm trying to find the right person for the job," he said simply. "You want someone who's experienced, honest and fair, don't you?" he asked her.

"That would be ideal," she returned evenly, and he knew he was going to hear more about this later. They did have to talk it out because he'd have to set up an appointment soon. A month wasn't all that long to finish what he had to do here, and then be on his way.

"I'd better be going," Seth interjected. "I have to drop off the pup for Molly around dawn tomorrow. Amanda insists she wants her there under the tree when Molly wakes up."

After a few more minutes of small talk, Seth hugged Kylie again, to Brock's consternation, and then left the vestibule. Brock noticed Kylie looked after him.

"What are you thinking?" he asked.

Startled that he'd noticed, she answered, "He works too hard. He needs a partner so he can take some time for himself."

"If he had more time, maybe he'd be spending it with you."

"Brock, I told you before that we're—"

"Yeah, you told me that you're friends. Lots of involvements get started with friendship."

"I once thought that was a good thing," she confided. "I knew Alex for so many years. But that didn't help *us*, did it?"

Even tonight, or especially tonight, she was thinking about Alex. He shouldn't be surprised.

The steps were cleared of snow as Brock and Kylie exited with Garrett, Gwen, Tiffany and Amy. But he stayed close by her. As they walked around the side of the church to the parking lot, snow started to fall.

Kylie extended her ungloved hand, letting the flakes land on her palm. "It's a shame I can't catch them," she joked. "But I guess if I caught them, I'd examine them too closely. That's the beauty of snowflakes. You have to see them while they're falling. Or in that one instant they land and then disappear."

"Philosophical tonight, are we?" Garrett asked, warm affection in his tone.

Kylie laughed. "I have more time to be philosophical these days."

In the parking lot, Gwen and Tiffany both gave Brock Christmas Eve goodbye hugs and Garrett extended his hand. "Merry Christmas."

Although Brock was surprised by the fact, he felt as if he'd known Garrett, Gwen and Tiffany longer than he had. Had he really somehow slipped into that circle Kylie had mentioned?

Once they were in the new truck and headed back to the ranch, Brock glanced at Kylie. "Go ahead."

"Go ahead?" she asked ingenuously.

"Yeah. I'm sure you have something to say about me searching for a real estate agent."

"Apparently I don't have to say anything. Have a guilty conscience?"

"No."

"Well, then, if you haven't learned to respect my opinion yet, if you didn't feel I'd be a helpful part of the process, then I guess there's nothing to say. Is there?"

"This has nothing to do with my respecting your opinion. I thought I'd just do some of the footwork for you while I was in town."

"I'm not going to argue about this, Brock. Not tonight. But let me tell you this. Alex cut me out of a lot of decisions that had to do with his life, mine and the ranch. The ranch is mine now. I'm responsible for it. Just as I'll be responsible for it after you leave. If there's a decision to be made, don't think you're going to do it on your own under the heading, 'For Kylie's own good,' because *I'm* going to take care of my own good."

With a sigh, Brock thought about those fifty head of Angus. When he presented her with the bill of sale, she might stuff it down his throat. That didn't matter. She needed them to get the ranch going again. She'd see that eventually.

He hoped. He didn't want to leave Saddle Ridge with a rift between them. He didn't need more regrets to carry along with him.

Since they hadn't returned from Christmas services until almost 1:30 a.m., Kylie was a late riser on Christmas morning. After her shower, she dressed in a green maternity top and slacks, and took Brock's present from her closet.

As soon as she came into the hall, she smelled the coffee and toast. Bacon, too? Had he waited for her to have breakfast?

Descending the steps, Brock's present in her hand, she

suddenly felt as if it were inconsequential. A pair of socks, for goodness sakes. He could buy dozens of pairs of socks if he wanted.

Sunlight streamed through the kitchen windows. It was reflecting off the snow outside and seemed twice as bright. Brock was taking bacon from a frying pan.

"Merry Christmas!" she said cheerily, hoping they could put aside any differences they had to have a peaceful day.

"Merry Christmas!" he returned with a slight smile. "Did you actually sleep last night?"

"I guess the baby got tired out by the services and singing. I actually did get a good night's sleep."

"Well, come on, then. Breakfast is ready. And I have a surprise for you afterward."

"A surprise as in—"

"A surprise as in—you'll just have to wait and see."

So she waited. Throughout breakfast they talked about Gwen's wedding coming up in a couple of days, the New Year's Eve celebration in town, how Molly would love her pup.

Finally when they were finished breakfast, Brock directed her, "Put on long underwear, heavy socks and boots."

"Are we going hiking?" she asked with a laugh.

"Nope. Not in your condition. It'll take me about fifteen minutes to get this ready. Is that enough time for you?"

"That's fine." She was thinking about her parka and not being able to get it zipped. She'd just have to put on plenty of layers.

Going to the pantry closet, he took out a large box wrapped in red foil and green ribbon. "You're going to need this for our excursion."

With trembling hands she took the box from him and found it heavy. Setting it on the table, she removed the bow and then the paper. When she lifted the lid, she gasped at what she found inside. Unfolding the wrap, she saw a hooded red wool cape lined in black velvet. "Oh, Brock, you shouldn't have."

"Don't say it and don't think it. I knew you wouldn't invest in a coat to get you through your last weeks of pregnancy. Well, this will work now and later. Seemed like a good idea to me."

Her eyes filled with tears. Setting the cape on the table in its box, she went to him and hugged him. There was so much emotion in the hug. It was filled with gratitude, but so much more than that. "How can I ever thank you for all you've done?"

"You don't have to thank me," he replied gruffly, wiping away her tears with his thumbs. "It's Christmas. I wanted to give you something you'd remember and be able to use, too."

"Remember?"

"That's the second part of my present."

"I have a present for you, too, but it's…it's small."

"A present is a present. It doesn't matter if it's big or small."

Crossing to the living room, she picked up the box and brought it to him. In a few moments he had the package opened. Inside, he saw the socks and smiled. "Did you make these?"

She nodded. "When I did your laundry, I didn't see any wool socks. If you put them on top of your others when you're in the barn, they should keep your feet warm."

"Thank you, Kylie. They're just what I need. I'll put them on now because I need to keep my feet warm this morning. If you have wool socks, you'd better wear them, too."

He was making the smallness of the gift unimportant, and she loved him for that, along with everything else. The cape was way too extravagant, but it was obviously a gift he had wanted to give her and she wouldn't make light of it. Or reject it. Not with him smiling at her that way. Not with that almost joyful look in his eyes that she didn't see there often. Maybe today they could forget about everything…except Christmas.

When he went to the sofa, he sank down on it and pulled off his boots, slipping the socks over the ones he was wearing. He grinned at her. "Perfect fit." Then he pulled on his boots once more.

When he stood, they just gazed at each other for a few moments, and neither seemed to know what to say. After he approached her, he tipped up her chin and kissed her forehead.

"Fifteen minutes," he said huskily. Then he grabbed his sheepskin jacket and went outside.

Fifteen minutes later, Kylie was ready. She'd donned a double layer of sweaters, put on her heaviest pair of slacks and two layers of socks.

As she stood on the front porch in her new cape, she couldn't believe what she saw. There was Brock at the end of the walk with a horse-drawn sleigh! She knew her smile was as wide as her face.

As she hurried down the path, Brock warned her, "Careful."

At least three inches of snow had fallen on top of what

hadn't melted from before. Brock had cleared the concrete for them and she could walk on the bare spots.

When she reached the sleigh, he said, "I thought we needed something special to do today."

All she wanted to do was throw her arms around him. This gift was so thoughtful, all of her words lodged in her throat and she couldn't get them out.

Tethering the reins to a cedar near the walk, he came very close and before she knew it he'd swept her up into his arms.

Laughing, she held onto his neck. "I could have climbed in."

"Maybe. But if I put you in the sleigh myself, I know you won't fall."

The sleigh was black, the seat for two upholstered in red leather. Bells were attached to the reins and she felt as if she'd stepped into a Christmas card. Sun glittered off the snow, stretching for miles as the crisp, cold air brushed around her.

"I was hoping the wind wouldn't be too bad today or this wouldn't have worked. I didn't want to give you frostbite."

After he climbed in beside her, he jiggled the reins, the bells jangled and they were off.

"Where did this come from?"

"A guy in town has about five of them. He rents them. When he delivered it the other day, I was hoping you wouldn't come outside. I've kept it in the storage shed covered in tarps."

"It's a wonderful surprise. You went to a lot of trouble."

"I thought we both needed to make a new memory on Christmas Day." Brock had tossed two blankets into the sleigh and he insisted she cover up with them.

The ride was exhilarating and exciting...and joy-filling.

Except for thoughts of her baby, she hadn't experienced true joy since way before Alex had died. It seemed she had been constantly distracted by their problems and how to work them out. But today, she almost felt free.

That was because of Brock and the stability he'd brought back into her life. Was she mistaking gratitude for deeper feelings?

Glancing over at him, his profile backlit by the sun, she knew she felt a whole lot more than gratitude.

"When I was in town earlier this week at the feed store," Brock commented, "John Bartholomew told me mustangs were spotted in the Painted Peaks."

John was Shaye's brother, and Kylie knew he was a reliable source.

"One band or more?" The mustangs roamed in bands that were their families.

"He said one band of four was spotted."

"Do you know where?" Excitement filled her that the mustangs had returned to the mountains here.

"Near Wild Horse Canyon."

"Can we go see them?"

Brock laughed. "I knew you'd ask that. We probably can if we don't get more snowfall. If the weather's good tomorrow, we can try it. But if we can't see them from one of the fire roads, forget hiking."

She laughed. "I'll be satisfied to use binoculars."

"Until spring," he murmured.

In some ways, he did know her well. Yep, after the baby was born, she'd be near the canyon—hiking, observing, learning.

"Is that cape warm enough?" he asked.

Brushing the hood back a little, she assured him, "It's perfect."

Their gazes met and she knew today was a day they'd both always remember. She loved this man in a way she'd never loved Alex. That thought filled her with guilt. It also made her wonder, if anything developed between her and Brock—really developed—could she make a relationship work? Would she even consider jumping into marriage when her last had been so disastrous?

Pulling her gaze from Brock's, she looked out over the open fields. She was an idiot for even thinking about marriage when Brock wouldn't even abide the thought of staying.

Any dreams she entertained had better concern her baby, not Brock. Or when he left, she'd be devastated.

When he left, the bottom was going to fall out of her world. There was nothing she could do about that.

Chapter Ten

Kylie remembered the rush of wind against her face, Brock's solid body beside her as she started dinner after their sleigh ride. Both the sleigh ride and the cape he'd given her showed her he cared. But how much did he care? After she finished in the kitchen, she sat on the sofa to take off her boots. The front door opened and Brock came inside. "Something smells good," he said with a smile.

"I braised a brisket. It's simmering."

When his dark eyes found hers, she knew the brisket wasn't the only thing that was simmering. They ignored the chemistry between them. They tried to deny it. They tried to work around it. But it was there, whether they were outside or indoors. The problem was that not only was Alex a barrier between them but so was her love for Saddle Ridge. The ranch was a barrier because Brock saw it as a prize he could never attain. His father hadn't let him.

Until Brock could let go of that hurt, Kylie knew he'd never be happy. Saddle Ridge just reminded him of all of it, and so did she.

Breaking eye contact, he took off his coat and hung it in the foyer closet. Then he came to sit beside her as she absently rubbed one foot.

"Still cold?"

She hadn't felt cold while she was in the sleigh skimming over the snow, loving just sharing the experience with Brock. But as she'd returned to the house, she'd realized how cold her nose, fingers and toes were. Her nose and fingers had warmed up as she'd moved about the kitchen. But her feet...

Nodding, she responded, "I can't seem to get my feet warm."

Crossing to the fireplace, he opened the screen, touched a match to the wood he'd already positioned there and watched as it crackled to life.

When he came to the sofa, he sat near the arm and patted his legs. "Swing around. Put your feet up here."

Although she didn't know exactly what he intended, she did know if he were going to touch her this probably wasn't a good idea. Still, she simply couldn't resist. She'd shed one of her sweaters but was still wearing both pairs of socks. Now he peeled them from one foot and laid them on the end table. Then his large hand was covering her cold skin, and more than her foot was getting warm.

"That feels so good," she murmured.

Keeping one hand along the side of her foot, he stroked it with his other. "Do you need help preparing dinner?"

"Not really. Unless you want mashed potatoes rather than baked. We'll have to peel."

"I can do that."

"I made a chocolate cake with peanut butter icing yesterday."

His eyebrows arched. "How did I miss that?"

"Maybe because I stowed it in the laundry room where it will stay cooler."

"You just didn't want me to get at it before today."

She laughed, but the laugh soon faded into a contented purr as his fingers did delicious things to her feet. His thumbs stroked up the arch of her foot, massaged the heel, then slid to the instep.

After a few minutes he said, "I think this one's warm." He slipped a sock back on and worked on her other foot.

His thighs were taut, powerful and muscular under her legs. Today he was wearing a navy flannel shirt with a black T-shirt underneath and black jeans. She was overwhelmed by her desire to wrap her arms around him, lay her head against his chest, stroke his jaw. She could imagine them together so easily.

Because she loved him? Because she'd finally accepted Alex's betrayal and what it had meant? Because, whether or not Alex had been willing to put their marriage back together or not, she had doubts that he ever could have given up the rodeo life he loved to stay at home and be a husband and dad?

Brock, on the other hand...

He must have felt her staring at him. When he looked at her, there was so much turmoil there, she could hardly stand to see it.

"I shouldn't even be touching you," he said gruffly.

"Why did you offer?"

His hands fell from her feet as he blew out a sigh. "I want to do a hell of a lot more than rub your feet. I chose that to pacify myself."

Shifting her feet from his lap, she let them drop to the floor and moved over next to him. "You don't want to feel anything for me."

"You were Alex's wife."

"Alex is gone," she said softly.

"No. No, he's not, Kylie. That's the crux of it. Tell me something. Do you feel Jack in this house?"

"Not anymore."

"Well, I do. I'm sleeping in his bedroom, for God's sake."

"When you were a kid, it wasn't a bedroom," she offered, hoping to make him see he was dwelling on something he shouldn't dwell on.

"No, it wasn't. But I still came home after he had his heart attack. Not often, but now and then. I remember one visit when he was getting feebler. I went in to spend some time with him, to try and have a conversation with him. He asked me about my work. I told him I liked the new horse Alex had bought. And that was the end of it. There was no meeting of minds. There was no attempt at reconciliation. He could have cared less if I left and didn't come back. I *didn't* come back again, not until his funeral. I can remember every heartbeat of silence in that room. Every awkward moment. Every word I was thinking but didn't say."

She slipped her hand into his, not caring if she should or shouldn't. He closed his fingers around hers.

Close to him now, she could see the lines around his eyes. Were they from squinting into the sun? Or from

worrying too much that he wasn't good enough to be Jack's
son? Jack had been prejudiced against Brock because he
was Apache. His mother had been good enough to sleep
with, but not good enough to make a life with. But because
of his heritage, not in spite of it, Brock was a man of in-
tegrity. She loved that most about him. Yet he, too, had a
blind spot. He might have resented and hated Jack Warner
at times, but he'd loved Alex and this ranch. Alex had had
true affection for him, too, but that had gotten muddled in
the way Jack had treated them both.

At this moment, she didn't care about Jack or Alex, or
memories that Brock couldn't shift away. She cared about
the two of them and what they could have. Dare she even
think about it? Dare she hope that someday Brock could
put all the bad memories aside?

Suddenly he said, "Damn it, Kylie. You're just too beautiful today. Don't look at me like that."

The fact that he thought she was beautiful when she was
this pregnant said a lot. When his arm went around her, she
leaned closer to him. Her heart coaxed her to tip up her
chin…to invite him to kiss her. She knew he was a strong-
willed man with plenty of self-control. Maybe too much.
She also knew she was complicating her life even more
than it was.

Nevertheless, at this moment all she knew was that
she wanted to give in to her feelings for Brock. Could he
do the same?

When his lips pressed to hers, it was the dawn of Christmas again and she was unwrapping something beautiful.
His desire swept her into the throes of an elemental need
that she never imagined a pregnant woman could have.

She slid her hand into his hair, caressed his neck and breathed him in. He smelled like the outdoors…and Brock. While his tongue coaxed hers into a mating dance, his hand cupped her breast. Though still small, she was fuller than she'd ever been. Exquisite sensations shot through her, and when his thumb rimmed her nipple, she moaned into his kiss, trying to tell him exactly how he was making her feel.

But her acknowledgment of the pleasure he was giving her reminded them both how far they were going…what could happen next if they didn't stop.

Brock broke away, breathing hard.

She was having trouble getting her breathing under control, too.

Instead of watching the distance he always put between them fill his eyes again, she rested her forehead on his shoulder. "Don't say anything."

Sparks popped from the logs on the grate. A chunk of snow slid from the roof, melting in the afternoon sun. Brock's heart beat steady and sure under her ear.

She was aroused. She wanted more of him. Didn't he want more, too?

"How can you just stop like that? How can you just turn off what happens between us?" Her question was almost an accusation.

"You think it's easy, Kylie? If you drop your hand a little lower, you'll find out exactly where *I* was headed."

Her hand was resting near his belt buckle. She almost did what he suggested, just to see his reaction. "Are you trying to shock me?"

"No, I'm being honest with you. I'm a man, like any other man. I want satisfaction. But I know the price of it."

"You mean the heartache when things don't work out."

"Not only heartache, but the loss of friendship. The loss of a connection that had been good and then turned into something else. Intimacy does that. It changes everything." After a silent few moments, he asked, "Did you ever sleep with anyone but Alex?"

"No."

"So you've had no practice at recovering from an affair," he pointed out.

"An affair? You think that's what I want?"

Leaning back farther away from her, he studied her. "I'm not sure you know what you want. You have a lot of reasons to turn to me."

"You think I kissed you because Alex slept with another woman and I want to know I'm still kissable?"

"That's one reason."

"You have a list of others?" She leaned away from him now, too, hurt that he didn't understand what she was feeling.

"You were drowning, Kylie, and I was your life raft. You needed another hand. You needed someone with capital to invest. You needed—"

"Stop. Stop right there. I don't recall asking you to be a life raft. I don't remember calling you at all. Do you think I wouldn't have come to the decision to sell some of the land on my own?"

"Maybe. Maybe not. I think you would have run yourself into the ground first."

"No. You're wrong. Because I have a child to think of now. Ever since you came back, you've been acting as if I'm some kind of forbidden fruit."

"Everything about our chemistry together feels wrong.

Don't you see that? You're grieving. I'd be a first-class heel to take advantage of that."

"So you're going to take the moral high ground? Tell me something, Brock. Isn't there just a little bit of satisfaction that you get when you kiss me *because* I was Alex's wife?" As soon as she voiced the question, she wished she hadn't. As soon as she voiced the question, she knew she'd trod into territory that was dangerous and taboo.

Brock's jaw set. Rising to his feet, he said firmly, "We're going to stop this now before we both say things we're going to be sorry for."

"The moral high ground again? Or avoidance?"

"Sometimes avoidance is safer," he snapped.

"Sometimes avoidance causes more misery," she returned, her emotions in a turbulent squall. Why couldn't he admit it if he felt something for her?

Yet on the other hand, maybe what he felt was simply too complex to deal with. It was all wrapped up with his memories of Saddle Ridge, a rivalry with Alex that Jack had set up, an attempt to stay removed from anything or anyone who could hurt him more.

She bit her lower lip. "I'm sorry. I shouldn't have said what I did. I don't want to ruin today."

He ran a hand through his hair. "Nothing's ruined. I'm not going to storm out of here because you said something I didn't like."

Maybe she hadn't ruined the day, but the closeness she'd felt earlier was gone.

"I'm going to call my mother and wish her a merry Christmas. After that, maybe we can play Scrabble until dinner's ready. I saw the box in the closet."

"Sometimes Molly and I play."

"Great. Then that's what we'll do until dinner. I'll go to my bedroom to make the call."

Realizing he wanted privacy, she said brightly, "And I'll make a salad while you're doing that."

He nodded, then headed toward his bedroom.

Kylie's knees were a little wobbly as she pushed herself up from the couch and went to the kitchen, still feeling the effects of Brock's kiss. She wouldn't disturb their peace again today. She wouldn't ask questions she shouldn't. She wouldn't make observations Brock might not want to hear. But as she thought about the cost of peace, she realized she'd kept quiet much too long in her marriage. If she had been more honest, if she had said exactly what she was feeling…

Her marriage to Alex might have broken up sooner. Maybe that would have been best. Yet if she and Alex had separated, she wouldn't be carrying this baby now.

Some days, life was just too tangled to figure out.

As Brock headed the new truck toward the Painted Peaks the day after Christmas, he stole a glance at Kylie. She was wearing the cape he'd given her yesterday and seemed to really like it. But she'd been quiet ever since their…argument. After she'd called her mother, too, they'd played Scrabble most of the afternoon with Christmas carols playing in the background. As they'd eaten, she'd talked about Gwen's wedding…how her friend and Garrett had decided they didn't want a rehearsal, but rather an unscripted ceremony.

"What time is Gwen's wedding Thursday evening?" he asked now to cut through the silence.

"At seven. But I'll have to be there around six. We're going to dress in a room at the back of the church. Have you decided yet if you're going to go?"

Before Christmas Eve he hadn't been sure. But he felt as if a friendship of sorts had begun between him and Garrett, as well as between him and Dylan, so he felt comfortable in attending. "I'll take you and then go over to the Silver Dollar for a cup of coffee before the ceremony. I didn't bring a suit. Do you think a shirt and a bolo tie will be all right?"

"That should be fine. Gwen said there would be less than fifty guests, and they just want everyone to be comfortable and join in their happiness. The reception is in the social hall afterward."

Brock's cell phone suddenly beeped.

Taking it from his jacket pocket, he checked the window and saw the caller was a man in the exploration and development department of a company he'd worked for in the past. "I should take this," he said to Kylie.

"Go ahead."

Brock knew as soon as he reached the foothills of the Painted Peaks and started climbing, he'd lose his signal. For that reason, he pulled over to the shoulder of the road. Minutes later, he dropped the truck's gear into Drive and started off again.

Now Kylie was looking out the window and not asking any questions. He knew why.

After another five minutes and a few more miles, he casually mentioned, "It looks as if I'll be headed to Alaska in March for a few meetings."

Although his eyes were still on the road, he could finally feel her turn and look at him. "Your next job?"

"Possibly. Probably. I won't know until the initial meetings are over with."

They both knew he wasn't going to stay…that that idea wasn't even on the table. So why was there this strain between them? Maybe she was worried about how she was going to handle everything. But in the next couple of weeks he'd have papers ready for her to sign and she'd be able to see handling the ranch would be manageable the way he planned to set it up. He hadn't mentioned the Angus on Christmas because he hadn't wanted to add to the tension between them. He'd tell her about the cattle when he had everything else arranged.

After Brock had driven a few more miles into the mountains, he veered off the plowed, main road onto one still packed with snow. He stayed in the ruts of other vehicles that had passed through. "If this gets too rough, we'll turn back."

"I'm not made of glass," she said lightly. "I want to see the mustangs."

Brock almost sighed, wondering how one, small, pregnant woman could be packed with so much spunk.

Keeping his eyes on the mountains as well as the road, he suddenly stopped. "Up there." He pointed to a snow-covered crest on Kylie's side of the pickup.

"Oh, *look* at them." Her voice was almost reverent.

There were four mustangs standing on the small peak, as if they were a welcoming committee: a dark grey stallion with a pale grey face, powerful-looking against the snow covered peaks, two sorrel mares and a dun-colored foal.

"You think they'll take off if we get out?" Kylie asked with that breathless wonder that was so much a part of her whenever she dealt with horses.

"I'll try it first and come around to your side. I don't want you to slip."

This time she didn't argue with him.

After he got out, he didn't slam his door, just left it open. Rounding the hood slowly, he gazed up at the mustangs and saw they were watching him. Watching, not running…as if they were curious about his adventure into their territory, territory they'd reclaimed after years of being absent from it.

When he reached Kylie's door, he opened it. "Stand on the running board. I'll lift you down."

The snow was deeper outside of the ruts, and she did as he suggested. But then she said, "I can step down. Just give me your arm."

Looking into his eyes, he saw that she thought it would be awkward for him to lift her…because of the baby. The baby always seemed to be between them. Yet her pregnancy was a bond tying them together, too. It was ironic. Strange. Unsettling.

She took hold of his forearm. He held her other hand, too, and eased her down to the snow.

Gazing up into his eyes she murmured, "Thanks," but then took a quick step away from him into deeper snow toward the mustangs.

Reaching into the pickup, he snatched the binoculars. As he held them and focused, he took a few quick photos and then gave them to her.

She didn't say anything as she lifted them to her eyes and adjusted the focus for the best view of the mustangs. "They're just beautiful."

He heard in Kylie's voice, absolute, complete appreciation of the wild horses, their heritage and configuration, their courage in living and roaming and existing. He also heard the faint desire to want to take care of them. Yet she knew she couldn't. These were *wild* horses, created for the land. Created to roam. Created to be free. She'd adopted one because the government agency thinned the herd and she couldn't stand the thought of the horses homeless...or worse. Yet she knew these animals belonged here, just as she did.

They passed the binoculars back and forth a few times after he showed her how to snap pictures with them.

"Shaye told me Dylan has a pair like this. Do you use them in your work?"

"Sometimes. I automatically tossed them into my duffel before I flew out."

One of the sorrels walked up to the other. The foal joined them and the stallion stood alone, gazing down at them, taking their measure. Then he turned, bobbed his head and all four horses disappeared from the crest of the hill.

Kylie sighed. "I could have stood here all day, just watching them."

"We're lucky we saw them. They could have been any-where."

Suddenly the stallion reappeared on the crest. Blue sky framed him as the sun glinted off his coat.

Brock was holding the binoculars, and he raised them to take a picture he knew would leave an indelible impression, and an indelible memory—as so many did where Kylie was concerned.

As soon as he snapped the photo, the horse disap-peared again.

There were tears in Kylie's eyes when Brock looked at her.

"What's wrong?" he asked gently, though his own chest was tight.

"He was just so…so…magnificent. Yet so alone."

"He has his band."

"I know," she replied, giving him a weak smile. "I know. But it's winter and it's just the four of them. And…" She fluttered her hands. "You know how I am about horses."

Yes, he did know. "It's winter. And then it will be spring, and summer and fall. Now that they're here, more will join them. Soon the Painted Peaks' canyons will echo with the sound of hoofbeats again."

When he gazed into Kylie's eyes, he knew she was thinking about the mustangs. But she was also thinking about spring, and summer and fall. Her baby would be born…and he would be gone.

"Come on. It's cold out here."

This time he knew the easiest thing to do. He scooped her up into his arms and set her inside the pickup. When he extricated himself from her, her eyes were brimming with tears. She closed them.

Although it was difficult to do, he stepped away. When he shut her door, he knew driving up here with her today had been a mistake. He should have let Dylan bring her.

Or maybe even Seth.

He just knew he didn't want to feel the wrenching discomfort in his chest, the acid bite in his stomach, the unnerving disquiet that he was sure would follow him when he walked away from her and her baby.

Chapter Eleven

In her wedding gown, Gwen looked like a princess, Kylie thought as she adjusted the tulle of her friend's veil.

"You feeling okay?" Gwen asked, quickly turning around and undoing the straightening Kylie had just accomplished.

"Can't you hold still for two minutes?"

The three of them had arranged each other's hair in the dressing room and attached bathroom, then donned their gowns. Afterward Shaye had ventured out into the vestibule to find their flowers. Gwen had been fidgeting, pacing and powdering her nose for the tenth time in the last five minutes. She was absolutely stunning in the long-sleeved beaded bodice and princess-style chiffon skirt.

"Of course I can't stand still. I'm getting married and I'm about to say the most important words in my whole life. I can't wait to do it, that's all. And you didn't answer my question."

"I'm feeling great."

Now Gwen studied her with narrowed eyes. After a long perusal she admitted, "You look great. That mauve-velvet gown suits you beautifully. But you're too quiet, even for you. Let me guess what's on your mind. Brock, maybe?"

This was Gwen, a woman as close to her as a sister. Still, it was hard for Kylie to admit she was being foolish...hard for her to admit she wanted something she couldn't have. "Maybe I'm worried about my baby, labor and delivery. Maybe I'm worried about whether or not I should have him or her at home." Gwen would be back from her honeymoon the day after New Year's—in plenty of time to coach her. They'd have a practice run after she returned.

"You've already made that decision. I saw Wanda yesterday and she said the two of you were going to practice breathing techniques next week before you and I work together. I still think you're crazy that you want to give birth naturally. Believe me, when Garrett and I have a baby, I'm getting an epidural."

"Practicing, are we?" Kylie asked with a mischievous grin.

"As much as we can, and don't change the subject."

Kylie went to the upholstered chair that sat by the full-length mirror and lowered herself into it. With a month to go until her due date, she seemed to be tiring more easily. "Uh-oh," she murmured. "Maybe I'd better not sit. I don't want to get wrinkled."

"That material doesn't wrinkle. Sit if you need to sit, and tell me the truth about what's going on with you."

Finally Kylie accepted the inevitable, giving Gwen what she wanted. "I love Brock."

"Oh, honey," Gwen murmured, coming over to crouch

down beside her, her gown swishing around her. "Do you have any idea how *he* feels?"

"I think he cares about me. I think he might even be attracted to me, as crazy as that seems with me being pregnant." She thought about what happened when they kissed. What happened when they touched. "But he can't wait to leave. He has meetings in Alaska in March. He's going back to the life that he wants, and it doesn't include Saddle Ridge. Or me."

"Or memories of Jack Warner," Gwen added. "We were kids when all of that went on. But even *I* remember the talk. One time I went to Clementine's looking for my dad, afraid he was on a binge again. It was the day after high school graduation—*Brock's* high school graduation. Two men were sitting at the bar, talking to the bartender about how the high and mighty Jack Warner hadn't attended his older son's graduation. They bet money on the fact that in five years he'd be front and center at Alex's graduation."

"Brock never told me Jack didn't go." Her fingers automatically went to the chain around her neck, hidden by the high collar of her dress. She pulled it out and slid her fingers under the mustang charm. "Brock gave me this the night Alex and I graduated. It must have really hurt him to be there that night with Jack, watching Alex getting his diploma…watching his father being so proud of Alex."

"I remember that necklace. You used to wear it all the time until…"

"Until Jack's funeral when Brock attended it with his wife."

"Has he told you why his marriage broke up?"

"He and his wife wanted different things."

"There could be another reason he's determined to leave. Some men can't accept another man's child."

"I know. I almost think it would be better if he left before the baby's born. But he has a misguided sense of responsibility where I'm concerned. The thing is, I want every day I can have with him before he *does* leave."

The door to the dressing room burst open then, and Shaye came inside carrying a box with Gwen's bouquet, as well as hers and Kylie's. Gwen had asked Tiffany to be a member of the wedding party, too, but the young mother had insisted Kylie and Shaye should share that honor because they had been friends for so long. Besides, Tiffany wanted to watch the wedding ceremony with Amy and keep her baby happy.

"Does Garrett ever look handsome in that Western-cut tuxedo!" Shaye remarked.

She stopped when she saw Gwen crouched down next to Kylie. "Is everything okay?"

Kylie pushed herself up out of the chair. "Our very best friend is getting married to the man she loves. Everything is more than okay. Come on, Gwen, you can primp one last time before you take your dad's arm." Her father was sober now, had been for the past few years. Everything was right in her friend's world.

No matter what was going on in Kylie's life, this night belonged to Gwen. She would do everything in her power to make sure the ceremony went off without a hitch.

Brock's shirt collar felt tight as the wedding march began to play, and he didn't know why he was so damned uncomfortable. Was it because the music reminded him of his own wedding day? He hadn't attended Alex and Kylie's ceremony. He and Marta had been consulting on a project in the Middle East.

Standing along with everyone else, he noticed Shaye walk down the aisle first. Beside Dylan, he saw the look of pride on the man's face as his wife, carrying a bouquet of pink roses intertwined with lace and ribbons, began the procession. Although Brock knew Kylie would be next, he wasn't prepared for the impact of seeing her in the pinkish velvet gown, some of her hair braided with ribbons, a glow on her face because she was happy for her friend. Pregnant or not, she was the most beautiful woman he'd ever seen.

A whisper in his head asked, *What if she'd be willing to leave Saddle Ridge? What if she'd give it all up for you?*

Kylie will never leave Saddle Ridge, he answered back. The ranch and the horses and the Painted Peaks are in her blood. Any money she'd receive from selling it would never replace the emptiness she'd feel if she left it. He knew her that well. He also knew more than the ranch was standing between them. Alex's baby. He felt like a jerk for thinking it, but the only way he wanted Kylie was free and clear of Warner ties.

But you're a Warner, that whispery voice insisted.

He'd spent his whole life fighting against that fact.

When Kylie drifted past him, they made eye contact. Her smile was tremulous. His was forced.

After she passed by him, he still watched her. When she took her place beside Shaye, they both waited for the bride. He waited, too, knowing the ceremony would be over soon...knowing his time at Saddle Ridge was coming to an end.

* * *

The real estate agent's office was an eight-by-eight cubicle that made Kylie feel claustrophobic. Her chair was against the wall, Brock's chair close beside her. Linda Torrence, a pretty blonde, sat across from them at a large desk. If the desk had been smaller, they all might have had some breathing space.

"I'm so glad you decided to use our agency," Linda said. "This is a first for me, signing a client before the First Night celebration begins." She looked at Kylie now. "But Mr. Warner said it would be convenient for you since you were coming to town anyway."

It was true, Brock had set everything up. Together they'd studied agents' credentials and had chosen one. Brock asked if Kylie could sign the papers tonight, deciding it would be convenient to have their meeting before they met Shaye and Dylan for the concert in the town hall. After the concert they'd go to the Silver Dollar for the dessert bar several establishments were sponsoring. The object of Wild Horse's First Night Celebration was to give residents several places to gather until everyone lined the streets at midnight to watch the mustang run through town.

Linda had already given them a presentation on what she thought she could do for them, showing them similar properties and acreage and how much they sold for, calculating comparison values in Wild Horse Junction and in nearby Cody.

Now she slipped all the computer generated printouts into a folder and laid it before them. "I think I've covered everything."

Although Kylie knew that Linda was a top-selling agent,

she wanted to know more about her. "How long have you lived in Wild Horse?" Kylie asked her.

"Eight years now. Each year I fall more in love with it."

"You sold real estate before you moved here?"

"Oh, yes. I've been selling since I was twenty-one. I grew up in the Chicago area."

"What made you move here?"

"Your husband didn't tell you?"

Kylie's gaze jerked to Brock's and then back to Linda's. "My husband?"

"Yes. Isn't that why you came to me? Because Alex mentioned me before he...before he died?"

This was a turn Kylie had never expected the conversation to take. When she glanced at Brock again, she saw he was just as surprised as she was.

In fact, he interjected now, "I didn't know Alex had come to you. I made comparisons of agents in the area on the computer, and you were one of the top three. After asking around, I learned you had a good reputation. That's why we're here."

"Oh. I see."

"When did Alex consult with you?" Kylie asked.

"About a year ago. The beginning of last December, it was. You didn't know about that?"

"No, I didn't," Kylie admitted.

"We didn't go further than preliminary talks. He wanted to find out what he could get for Saddle Ridge."

"He was going to sell the entire ranch?" Kylie absolutely couldn't imagine it. She couldn't imagine Alex thinking about doing it, let alone doing it and not telling her. Well, she was learning *that* had come to be the norm.

Brock leaned forward, his arm brushing hers. "Did Alex have his eye on someplace a little smaller?" he asked now.

"No, not at all." Linda's gaze fell on Kylie. "He just said the ranch was becoming a burden for the both of you. With the money you could get for it, you could travel with him from rodeo to rodeo for a long time, and not have to worry about taxes or expenses or the price of beef. He was very honest about it." Linda continued, "That's why I was a bit disappointed when you said you were only interested in selling part of the back acreage. But that *is* prime property, and as I told you, we should do quite well."

After that, Kylie concentrated hard on every form Linda put before her to sign. She read every word, made sure she understood what kind of advertising the agency was going to do on her behalf. Although Brock watched over her, posed a question of his own now and then, for the most part he didn't interfere and let her handle the transaction.

Finally as Linda gathered all the papers together, though, he said, "So why *did* you move to Wild Horse Junction?"

"Because I heard that rodeo cowboys still lived here. A little fantasy of mine, but I always wanted to date a cowboy."

Kylie couldn't help but wonder if Alex had made a pass at Linda, maybe offered to date her himself. But there was nothing in Linda's demeanor that would suggest that.

Brock was the one who asked, "*Did* you date a cowboy?"

"Actually, Alex introduced me to one of his friends. He's a calf-roper and has a place outside of town. Jeff Mitchell. We're still dating."

Kylie knew Jeff. He and Alex sometimes traveled the circuit together. Older than Alex, he'd always been quiet around her. So Alex had been a matchmaker, too?

Brock checked his watch. "Finished. With time to spare before the concert."

"Listing with us is pretty cut-and-dried," Linda said, standing. "But when offers start coming in, that might require some negotiation. On the other hand, we can hope for two at the same time and let them bid against each other."

Five minutes later, Brock had helped Kylie with her cape and they were walking along the street to the town hall, both of them silent.

Finally, Kylie said, "I don't know whether to laugh at the idea that Alex thought I would follow him from rodeo to rodeo, or to be furious with him for it."

"It was probably his fantasy."

She gave Brock a sharp look. "Some fantasy, driving from city to city, never having a home. How could he even think about doing something like that?"

"Saddle Ridge is simply a house, barns, outbuildings and some land. Apparently, Alex wasn't sentimentally attached to it."

"You mean like I am?" she asked defensively, feeling as if he were attacking all she held dear. "Saddle Ridge became my home when I didn't have one. I had to sell my pop's place. Do you know how hard that was to do? Do you know how many tears I shed going through room after room, time after time, wishing I didn't have to sell it yet knowing I did? I *felt* my dad there. I felt my mom there. I had to sell all the horses except Caramel. When my mom came back here those couple of months to oversee every-thing, even *she* cried, and she couldn't wait to leave the place. It had been home to her, too. She and Pop were new-lyweds there. She was pregnant with me there. It's more than sentimentality, Brock, and if you don't understand it, I can't explain it."

"Oh, I understand it. But you've got to realize something. Your mother left because she wanted a different life. Alex thought about selling because he apparently did, too. Saddle Ridge was a burden to him because he didn't know how to handle it."

Actually sounding as if he would have approved, she was totally frustrated with Brock. Her turmoil pushed her to walk faster.

He caught her arm. "We have plenty of time. You don't have to rush."

"Always the practical one," she said, almost angrily.

He released her arm. "Somebody has to be."

That was the end of their conversation until they found Shaye and Dylan outside of the town hall waiting for them.

In the town hall's reception room, where everything from town meetings to dances were held throughout the year, the residents of Wild Horse Junction were serenaded by a choir, solo artists and talented town musicians. When there was an intermission, Kylie was glad for the opportunity to stand up and walk around a bit. She wandered toward the historic building's vestibule, intending to peek outside to see if crowds were congregated yet for the midnight mustang run. All ages gathered because it was simply an exciting event.

Sidestepping around a group of concert-goers, Kylie came face-to-face with Trish Hammond.

At first, Kylie froze. Trish was the last person she wanted to see anywhere…ever. Then, with a sudden surge of face-the-world courage, she realized she wasn't the one who should be ashamed of anything. She wasn't the one who should be embarrassed. She wasn't the one who had done anything wrong.

Feeling a presence beside her, she knew it was Brock. She did *not* need his protection. "Go away," she murmured.

But, of course, he didn't.

Trish's surprise soon turned her smile into a coy one. "If you don't want him, I'll take him. I suppose one Warner's as good as another."

Everything inside of Kylie turned red. Her anger couldn't even be described. She knew Alex was as responsible for his part in the affair as Trish, and they were both to blame. But the woman had no right to put into words the one thing that was between her and Brock and might always be between them.

"I'll settle this," Kylie said, looking up at Brock.

"We both have something to settle."

Trish looked from one of them to the other. "You told her, didn't you?"

"I'm here, Miss Hammond," Kylie stated firmly. "Don't talk around me. Yes, Brock told me that Alex broke off his relationship with you to come back to me. Why are you so surprised? Aren't the very qualities you hooked onto with Alex the ones that made him turn away from you? Although he was reckless and impulsive and danger seeking, he *cared.* He cared about people and he cared about me."

"He cared about you so much he wanted to be with me any chance he could," Trish answered boldly.

Kylie realized this encounter wasn't worth the stress to her and her baby. "I don't know what has made you the vindictive woman you are. Maybe you just need some maturity. If you had been mature enough, maybe you would have seen that Alex was running. Not running from me and our marriage, but all the responsibility it entailed. He'd never learned how to deal with responsibility, and you were just a fix that let him avoid it."

This time Kylie could see that she'd struck home and now all of her anger deflated. She did *not* want to be like Trish. She didn't want to hurt this woman, even though Trish had hurt her. She simply wanted it all to end. "We live in the same town. We're going to run into each other from time to time, just like tonight. I surely won't be able to smile at you as if I mean it. Not for a long time. But I don't want to have this kind of conversation again, either. Do you?"

After studying Kylie for a long time, Trish shook her head. "No. But I can't just forget about everything, either. You're going to have his baby. You'll be coming into town—" She turned away and Kylie guessed Trish's eyes had filled with sudden tears. "Anyway," she went on, taking a deep breath, "I'm thinking about leaving Wild Horse. I have a friend in Billings who said I could make more money up there. So you won't have to worry about running into me much longer."

After a last, quick look at Brock, Trish exited the town hall and hurried up the street.

"You shouldn't have followed me out here." If Brock had stayed inside, Trish wouldn't have made the comment she had.

His answer was quick in coming. "You're not that far from your due date. Anything could happen."

"And you hope it will, don't you? So that you can take

me to the hospital. So this baby will be born and you can leave that much sooner."

"Kylie…"

"Don't." She held up her hand. "I've had enough of a roll-er-coaster ride tonight. I just want to see the mustang—be-cause when he runs through town I'll know it's a new year and a new beginning for me. The rest won't matter anymore."

A half hour later Kylie stood beside Brock in the shelter of the feed store's awning so aware of the man she loved she could hardly keep her attention on the New Year's celebration.

The high school band marched down Wild Horse Way and found their place by the town hall where it had been cleared for them. The mayor came next, driving his pickup, leaning out the window with his megaphone, wishing everyone a happy New Year. Finally, a minute before midnight, the band launched into their rendition of "Auld Lang Syne" as the sheriff and his deputies made sure the crowd was off the street and on the sidewalk.

Then the starter pistol went off, and Kylie listened for the thudding of hooves. Cora Wilke, one of Wild Horse Junction's barrel racers, sped down Wild Horse Way on a galloping chestnut mustang with a black mane. Church chimes sounded above the music. The mustang's thudding hooves faded away, and Kylie prepared herself to face the New Year. Soon she would be a mother and she just couldn't wait. Brock would leave…and she had to make peace with that.

After Brock parked the truck in one of the sheds, he went inside the house expecting that Kylie had gone up to her room. However, there she was, sitting on the sofa with a mug of tea in her hands.

"I was cold," she said simply. "If I don't get warmed up, I won't fall asleep."

"I could heat a brick in the oven," he said, trying to lighten up the atmosphere.

"I haven't tried that yet, though I *do* use a hot water bottle. It works."

If he were in bed with her, she'd be plenty warm. If he were in bed with her—

He'd been aroused all night, cold or no cold, confrontation with Trish Hammond or not. It was a condition he was getting used to around Kylie. At first, he'd denied it. Then fought it. Then tried to control it. Tonight he was feeling reckless. He was tired of the guilt and recriminations because maybe part of him wanted her *because* she'd belonged to Alex. He was tired of weighing the right thing against the moral thing. He had enough of "should he" or "shouldn't he." Did it matter that she'd trade one Warner for another? Did it matter that he was second instead of first?

If they both satisfied their curiosity and cravings, where was the harm?

They both knew the score. They both knew he was leaving.

Suddenly, as if maybe she could read his thoughts and was frightened by them, she stood. "I think I'll take this up with me."

"Good idea. I'll make a mug of hot chocolate to warm *my* toes."

Hesitating a moment, she looked down at her tea, then finally said, "I'll see you in the morning."

They smiled politely at each other, and that was the end of New Year's Eve.

Or so he thought.

Maybe she was thinking there wouldn't be many more mornings, because as she turned, he thought he saw the sheen of tears in her eyes. But she was gone so fast, he knew he'd never be sure. Kylie was like that. All emotion one minute, all action the next.

He made his hot chocolate and was sipping at it when Kylie called down the stairs. "Brock, I forgot something down there. My nightgown and robe are on the dryer. Would you bring them up?"

He'd seen her doing wash earlier in the day. Some of his clothes were in the laundry room, too. "Sure."

Dumping the rest of his chocolate into the sink, he rinsed the mug and put it in the dishwasher. Then he went to the laundry room. Two of his flannel shirts lay on a pile with her gown and robe. They were flannel, too—practical here in the winter. Noticing the ruffle around the neck of the nightgown and embroidery on the robe, he thought, *Practical, yet feminine.* Just like she was.

Grabbing the pile, he switched off the lights and then headed up the stairs.

He didn't mean to barge in on her. It was nothing like the night *she'd* barged in on *him*. After all, she was just unclasping her necklace.

What necklace was she wearing? He hadn't noticed anything lying on her sweater. Then he saw the mustang dangling from the chain.

Tossing the clothes he'd carried upstairs onto the bed, he approached her. He remembered her graduation night, the things he'd felt that he shouldn't have felt. "Is that the necklace I gave you?"

She didn't hesitate. "Yes, it is."

He wrapped his arms around her then, brought her closer and kissed her, much more provocatively than he'd kissed her that night so long ago. Much more provocatively than he'd ever kissed her before.

From Kylie's fervent response he knew tonight simply kissing would never be enough.

Chapter Twelve

Whatever Kylie had felt for Brock before became deeper, fuller, richer when he kissed her. The kiss was nothing short of explosive and she gave herself up to the power of it…to the power of her feelings for this man. Leaving the previous year behind, she thought about new beginnings. But most of all, she simply felt tonight.

Although Brock's kiss was possessive and claiming, his hands were almost gentle as they stroked up and down her arms, then went for the hem of her sweater. She didn't think about who she was, or how she looked, or how Brock saw her. Lost in the experience of simply wanting to love him, she let him undress her as she undressed him. She'd never touched him this intimately before with this much freedom. The night gave her freedom. The New Year gave her freedom. Her love gave her freedom.

By the time she'd rid him of his flannel shirt and T-shirt, he was skimming her slacks down her legs.

They were standing by the bed now, and as she reached for his belt buckle, he stayed her hands. "I'll get that. You crawl into bed."

The room was chilly and she knew he was thinking about that. Thinking about her. She slid under the covers waiting for him…yearning to touch him.

Moments later, he was beside her and they were facing each other. The dim light on the dresser still glowed and she was glad because she needed to look at him.

Under the covers, he wrapped his arm around her and began kissing her again. Her hands roamed his body as his roamed hers. His skin was hot, his spine straight.

When her hand rested on his backside, he groaned. "Do you know what you do to me, Kylie? Do you know how long I've wanted this?"

It seemed to her she'd wanted Brock for a lifetime. When he kissed her breasts and tongued her nipples, she knew she had. She belonged with him. She should have been his years ago. But time and circumstances and fate had intervened. She wanted to tell him she loved him, but he chose that moment to lay his hand on her tummy. He chose that moment to slide his fingers over her belly and her most intimate place. As he touched her there, she felt as if she was going to come apart in his hand.

After he stroked her, he probed deep with his fingers. She wanted him inside of her, but he didn't give her a chance to tell him that. The sensations he was initiating were so incredibly exquisite. She closed her eyes tight, held her breath and tried to absorb each one of them. At the same time he probed her, creating a rhythm as primitive as a drumbeat. His other hand, with one finger, touched the nub and sent off a flashpoint of tingles and erotic pleasure so strong, she called out and then cried his name.

She was still catching her breath when he started to turn away.

"Where are you going?"

"That was it, Kylie. That's what I set out to do. You're getting close to your due date."

All right, she was due in a few weeks. All right, she understood that maybe he didn't want to take any chances. But she would *not* let him pleasure her without her pleasuring him. So she took his arousal in her hands and felt the pulsing beat.

"Kylie." His tone was almost sharp.

She knew that was from arousal, frustration that she hadn't listened to him pliantly and a need he wouldn't admit.

When she stroked him, he sucked in a breath and said, "You don't have to…"

Pushing back the covers that were in the way, she touched the tip of her tongue to him. She was going to love him, and he would never forget it. Her fingers teased his stomach and her lips took him as her tongue laved him. He restlessly shifted with the growing pleasure. She touched him everywhere she could reach and she knew she was enhancing every sensation. His groans told her that. The expression on his face told her that.

She thought he was as far gone as she had been. She thought she'd been giving him the most pleasure he could ever experience. But suddenly, he turned from her, grabbed his shirt from the floor and covered himself with it. She watched as the pleasure she'd given him overtook him and he uttered a guttural cry. At that moment, she knew Brock hadn't accepted his feelings for her and believed she still belonged to someone else. If he could really embrace who he was, who she was and who they could be together, he would have climaxed inside her...he would have joined their bodies and known true union with her despite any practical concerns.

Lying beside him again, she pulled the covers over her to protect herself from the sudden chill. The wind sounded against the side of the house and whistled under the eaves.

After Brock blew out a long breath, he sat up and threw his legs over the side of the bed.

"You're just going to leave without a word?" Kylie asked, her voice trembling a bit.

"I never should have started that. I feel as if I used you and that was never my intention."

If she poured out her love for him, would it make a difference?

She knew it wouldn't. When he'd seen that necklace around her neck, he'd known what he meant to her. But to Brock, her love would never be enough. Even if she turned her back on Saddle Ridge. Even if she said she'd follow him anywhere. The truth was—she didn't know if she was willing to do that. Because she would still have Alex's baby to love, and she would never, ever hold back on that love. She would never, ever put her child in the position Brock had been in when he'd grown up at Saddle Ridge.

"I didn't feel used...until now," she declared.

Brock picked up his boots and the clothes that he'd

tossed by the side of the bed. Then he left her room without another word.

There was nothing more to say.

Winter raged the first two weeks in January, putting down more snow, creating extra chores for Dix and Brock. Frustrated that she couldn't help them, Kylie sat in her craft room working on a beaded comb for Lily on Sunday afternoon. She and Brock didn't have much to say to each other, and they were awkward when they were together.

The day Brock had taken her into town for a checkup with her doctor, she'd met with her midwife as well as her obstetrician. She was ready. Her midwife was ready. Gwen had said to call her anytime…anywhere.

Earlier Kylie had called her mother for a long talk. Her mom hadn't offered to come to Wyoming to help after the baby was born, but she'd invited Kylie to bring the baby to Colorado for a visit. It would be difficult, but somehow Kylie wanted to do that…to feel her mother's love again close-up, to see pride as her mom got to know her grandchild.

Even though Kylie had considered it, she'd decided not to go to church today. Her back ached a little from lifting the filled Crock-Pot this morning. Besides, Brock would want to drive her to church, and she couldn't abide the thought of another tense trip, another spate of silence where neither of them said what they were thinking. Getting through meals was bad enough, and even those Brock was avoiding. He'd grab something with Dix or make sure he was busy doing chores.

Midafternoon she was staring out the window trying to imagine her life in a few months, when Brock came into the room, a sheaf of paper in his hand. She thought maybe he needed to use the computer.

He was still wearing his coat, though, and she looked at him, puzzled. "Aren't you staying?"

"No, I'm going back out. Dix and I have to take out the wagon and lay out feed. More snow's coming tonight."

After he set the papers on the table, she pushed aside the comb she was working on. "What are these?"

"These are a conglomeration of things you need to know about. The first printout is a receipt. It's a bill of sale for fifty head of Angus. They'll be delivered at the end of March. I was going to give them to you for Christmas, but I knew you wouldn't accept them. Not along with the cape. They're just part of the package I'm leaving you with, so you can get Saddle Ridge going again."

A package he was leaving her with?

Words were on her tongue but she kept silent, waiting to see what came next. She set the bill of sale aside as she examined the second paper in the pile.

"That next sheet is an accounting of the capital I've added to your accounts. Even if you sell that parcel of land, you'll need that money for horses, supplies and expenses until you get everything up and running again. You don't need to pay me back. I don't want any argument on this. We're family. With this, you'll be on your feet again."

As if he were in a hurry, he went on, "The third sheet is a lease agreement for the sugar-beet farming. I found someone willing to take it over. You and he will split the profits. In a year you'll have that adding to your income. By then, Saddle Ridge will be a well-oiled wheel. You won't need to be depending solely on any one aspect of it. If you want to start breeding horses at that point, you can."

"How's Feather?" she suddenly asked.

Brock looked confused by her change of subject. "Feather's fine. By spring you should be able to put a saddle on her."

"Thanks to you. Thanks to your gentling. You liked working with her, didn't you?"

A neutral expression stole over his face that told her he wasn't going to let her see anything that he was feeling. "You started the process."

"And you continued it. You liked exercising Caramel, taking Rambo on runs. Admit it."

"That doesn't have anything to do with the rest of this."

"Sure it does, Brock. You love the land and you love the animals. I think part of you even loves Saddle Ridge. But you won't let yourself feel it. You're always running away from it."

"I haven't run away from it. I just found a different life."

"No. You found a life that won't remind you of your old one. There were things in that old life that mattered, too. Like me and Alex. Like the teepee rings."

That brought a startled expression to his face.

"You think I don't know about them?" she asked more gently. "You think I don't know that you've always spent time there?"

"So what if I have? I can find teepee rings other places in Wyoming. I can find Mayan ruins in South America. Remnants of the Athabascan heritage in Alaska. I can appreciate where man has come from anywhere."

"Don't generalize this, Brock. When I asked you if you wanted your mom to join us for Christmas, you said she'd never come back here. Is that really true? No ghosts remain. Sure, there are memories. But past memories can be changed into better ones…into good ones with new memories. Haven't we done that while you've been here?" She so wanted to pull his feelings from him…to make him admit what they had.

"Memories you and I made that we're going to regret. A clean break will be best this time, Kylie."

"And you're never going to see—" Her voice broke. She was going to say, "the child who could become your son or daughter." Instead, she said, "your niece or nephew?"

"You have enough people in your life. Your son or daughter won't miss me."

"*I'll* miss you."

His face hardened and she knew he was thinking about all the things he'd rescued her from. All the help he'd given her. But none of that was the reason she'd miss him. He wouldn't believe that, though. He wouldn't believe her love had begun long before her marriage to Alex. Because he didn't want to. He was still nursing wounds that would never heal unless he poured the salve of love on them.

She picked up the papers lying on the table. "I'll accept all of this for now. But you'll share in the profits and I'll repay you someday, Brock. I have my pride, too."

His eyes were black with all the emotion she guessed was rolling inside of him, but he simply said, "Yes, I guess you do. I'll be out with Dix for the next few hours."

"I made soup in the Crock-Pot, so it will be ready whenever you're finished."

She'd done it because she knew he couldn't miss dinner that way…he couldn't completely avoid her that way.

After a last look at the papers on the table, he left the room, walked down the steps and went out the front door.

Leaning back in her chair, she stared down at the gifts he'd given her.

There was one missing—his heart. He couldn't give it to her if it wasn't whole. Maybe someday…

She felt as if she'd been waiting all her life for Brock. She'd just have to wait a lifetime more.

Although the grey clouds seemed to meet the fence line, snow had not yet started falling as Kylie's phone rang.

When she answered it, Amanda Daily's voice was panicked. "Have you heard from Molly?"

"I talked to her on Wednesday."

"No, I mean *today*."

"No, I haven't heard from her. Why? What's wrong?"

"We can't find her. This is all my fault. If I had just told her like George wanted me to—"

"Told her what?" Kylie was afraid the couple was getting a divorce and had tried to keep that information hidden from Molly.

"I might lose the cell signal soon. I'm headed out to one of her friends where I think she might have gone. George is out of town with Seth, looking for a horse for her."

"Did you check the clinic?"

"That's the first place I went, but it's locked up tight."

"What happened?" Kylie asked again. She needed to know before Amanda drove out of range.

A few moments of silence ticked by until Amanda said, "Molly's adopted."

Adopted? She would never have thought it. Never

would have expected it. She knew Amanda and George Daily loved Molly deeply, richly, fully.

"George and I have been arguing about telling her for a few months. Finally, I decided when he got home today, we would tell her. So I got out her birth certificate and some papers I'd received—background on her biological mom, that kind of thing. I had them in my room on the dresser. Sometimes Molly goes in there to use a dab of my perfume. She must have seen them. I don't even know how she left the house without me knowing. I usually hear the door. Her coat and hat and boots and gloves are gone. And so is her puppy Buffy. She must have taken her with her. I checked for tracks, followed her boots and paw prints to the end of the street, and that was it. Snow is going to start falling any minute, and…" Amanda's voice started fading in and out. "I just hope…that her friends…explain…"

The call dropped and Kylie knew Amanda was out of range.

Standing still for a few moments, Kylie considered her options. Although Seth's clinic was locked up tight, that didn't mean Molly wasn't inside. Seth kept the key hidden behind a loose brick at the side of the building and Molly knew about that, just as she knew the security alarm code.

And if she weren't in the clinic?

There were a few other places in town Kylie knew the ten-year-old often liked to go if she wanted to be by herself. There was the gazebo in the park, a video arcade next to the pizza shop in the Plaza. She could take Buffy in there.

Knowing panic would do absolutely no good, also

knowing Molly had a good head on her shoulders, Kylie went to the kitchen for her boots. She slipped out of her moccasins and a sharp pain stabbed her back. She'd strained it this morning with the heavy Crock-Pot. That's all it was.

She tried to call Brock on his cell phone, but she couldn't get him. His voice mail picked up. If he were on the wagon behind a tractor hoisting hay into the pasture with the wind blowing against him, he wouldn't hear it. So she left a message. "Molly's missing and I can't just sit here. I think I know where she might be. I'm driving into town to look. First, I'm going to the clinic. She knows where Seth hides the key and she knows how to turn off the alarm. I'm betting that's where she is. I'm taking my cell phone with me, however good it is. If they really worked, I could get you now. Don't worry about me, I'll be fine."

She wanted to say so much more, but she didn't know how, and she didn't know if it would do any good. So she simply added, "I'll see you soon," and then hung up.

Ten minutes later she was on the road in the new pickup truck headed toward town. The pain in her back was getting worse, but she ignored it as best she could, concentrated on her driving as snow fell now, and heard a siren in the distance that told her there had been an accident or someone needed an ambulance. After she arrived at the clinic, she quickly parked in the space closest to the back door. A light layer of snow was covering everything, and she didn't want to slip.

Before she rounded the corner of the building she reached a Rocky Mountain juniper, pushed the limbs aside and found the brick she was looking for. A couple of times when Seth had to go out of town, she'd come in and tended to the animals for him.

Finding a fingerhold, she pulled on a corner of the brick and it slid out. But no key rested behind it. She checked the ground under it to make sure the key hadn't fallen. It hadn't. That meant Molly was probably inside.

As she pushed the brick back into its space, sharp pain lanced up her spine and she doubled over, hugging her tummy. The pain made its way around her middle. She realized now, heavy Crock-Pot or no, she was in labor. At that moment, water gushed from between her legs, right there at the corner of the veterinary clinic.

Calm. You've got to stay calm, she told herself. First, she had to get inside and make sure Molly was safe.

Lifting her purse from the ground where it had fallen when she'd doubled over, she went to the door and pounded on it. "Molly. It's Kylie. If you're in there, come open the door. I'm in labor."

If Molly were back in the kennel with the animals, she might not hear. Kylie pounded again, even harder, until her fist hurt. She called once more, "Molly, I'm in labor. Let me in."

A light went on and Molly opened the door, wide-eyed. "You *can't* be in labor. You're not due until the twenty-ninth."

Forcing a smile, Kylie slipped inside. "Tell the baby that, honey, because he or she isn't listening to *me*."

"What do you want me to do?" Molly asked, as her puppy came over to Kylie and sniffed around her boots.

"I don't want you to do anything. This is my first baby so it shouldn't happen fast. I'll have to time the contractions." She tugged on the ten-year-old's arm and pulled her toward a bench in the reception area. "Come sit with me and tell me what's going on with you."

"Shouldn't we call somebody?"

"I could be in labor for hours."

Sliding onto the bench, Molly stooped down to pet her pup. She mumbled. "Did you talk to Mom?"

"Yes, I did and she's worried sick." Kylie took her cell phone from her purse. "Can you tell me her cell number? I have to let her know you're okay."

"I'm not ready to go home yet."

"Molly." As she said the little girl's name, tightness began in her womb, curved around her tummy and took her breath away.

"Are you having another contraction?"

"Looks like I am," Kylie managed to say, breathing as the midwife had taught her.

"We've got to call an ambulance!"

"I'm going to time the contractions first. Use the land line and call your mother. Now, Molly. I'll try to call Brock on my cell. If I can't get him, maybe I can get Gwen or Shaye."

But neither of them had any luck.

"I tried Mom, but she's not answering. And Dad isn't home, either. I left messages for both of them."

The calls had taken a few minutes and another contraction began. Now Kylie became scared. Where was everybody today?

She remembered. Yesterday Dylan had driven Shaye and Timmy into Billings. He had a meeting there with the editor of a magazine. They had decided to take Timmy and make a family outing out of it. Gwen and Garrett, officially newlyweds now, could be anywhere, including in Garrett's outside hot tub. Tiffany and the baby could be visiting a friend. Kylie dialed the midwife.

At the midwife's chipper greeting, she said quickly, "Wanda, I'm in labor at the veterinary clinic."

"Why are you at the veterinary clinic?" the midwife asked, aghast.

"It doesn't matter. I think you should come. The contractions are less than five minutes apart."

"Are you alone?"

"No. Molly Daily, who's ten, is with me. Why?"

"Because I can't get to you. The road's closed at this end of town. There was an accident. I doubt if the ambulance will be available, either. I'm going to have to drive west and go over some side roads to get around to you. But I *will* get there. See if Molly can gather supplies for you. Tell her to find clean towels. I imagine Seth has those. Is there a cot or anything where you can stretch out?"

"I think there's a sofa in Seth's office."

"Good. Go in there and get as comfortable as you can."

Suddenly, Kylie's cell phone beeped, signaling another call coming in. Not that she knew how to take it. "Wanda, I'm on my cell phone and somebody's calling."

"Go ahead. If it's an adult and they can get to you, let them."

She'd left a message at Gwen's. Maybe her friend was calling back.

Pressing the button she used to answer the phone, she heard Brock's voice. "Kylie?"

There was no one else she'd rather talk to, even if he yelled at her. "I'm here...at the clinic. And I'm in labor."

There was a pause as if it took a second for the shock

to sink in. "I'm already on the road. I'll be there in five minutes. Thank God Dix souped up his truck. How bad are the contractions?"

"I've only had—" The next one took her breath away and she handed the phone to Molly.

As soon as Molly figured out who she was talking to, she gave Brock a blow-by-blow, which probably wasn't the best thing to do. Molly explained the call that Kylie had placed to the midwife.

After the contraction passed, sweat beaded on Kylie's forehead. She took the phone again and pushed herself up from the bench. "I'm going to Seth's office. I can lie down there."

"Don't fall," Brock warned her.

"I won't. I have Molly to lean on. We're okay, Brock. Really."

"As okay as a pregnant woman in labor can get," he muttered. "Damn it, Kylie, why couldn't you have stayed put?"

"Because I had to find Molly. And right now I want to talk to her. I'm going to click off. You'll be here soon. I need a few minutes alone with her."

She heard his sigh of frustration. "Okay. But don't click off the phone. Keep it in your hand and connected to me."

As Molly helped Kylie to the office, she asked, "Did Mom tell you I'm adopted?"

Kylie sucked in a breath but managed, "Yes, she did. Did you have any idea before today?"

"No. Never. Not even when my parents were arguing. But now I realize I don't look like either of them. I have blond hair and Mom has red. Dad has brown."

In the veterinarian's office, Kylie took off her cape and saw the afghan lying over the back of the sofa. Undressing from the waist down, she lay on the sofa and covered herself with the throw. "You're a smart girl, Molly. If you never suspected you were adopted, what does that tell you?"

For a few moments, Molly looked confused. Then she knelt down next to Kylie, her puppy close by her side. "I guess it means I never *felt* adopted."

"Exactly. Do you know *why* you never felt adopted? Because your mom and dad loved you so much—they *love* you so much—that there isn't any difference if you had been their baby or an adopted baby. They love you as their own. When you came to live with them they took you into their hearts and they've kept you there. All the tension you've been feeling the past couple of months, I imagine, came from them trying to decide what the best thing to do was. My guess is your mom was afraid you'd love her less if you knew the truth. Or you'd want to go find your real mother. And where would that leave her? Think about that, Molly. Think about how they've always taken care of you. How they've always loved you. You *are* theirs, in every way that matters."

Kylie heard something then and looked around Molly to see Brock standing in the doorway. "How are we doing?" he asked.

"We're doing—" The next contraction almost brought Kylie to a sitting position.

Hurrying inside, he tossed off his hat and quickly supported her with his arm around her shoulders. The contraction no sooner ended than the next one began.

Molly looked frightened, and the puppy beside her whined.

"This is going to happen sooner rather than later," Brock said briskly. "Molly, get me towels. Then I want you to take the pup with you and go to the waiting room. You can let the midwife in."

"Keep trying to call your mom and dad," Kylie said between clenched teeth. "And remember—"

Molly looked back at her. Then she said slowly, "I know. Remember…they love me." The pup trailed behind her as she went to find those fresh towels.

There was no hesitation in Brock as a few moments later he slid a towel under Kylie and stacked a few more beside the sofa. Then he spread her knees. "I have to check."

Kylie felt no embarrassment as he said, "I can see the baby's head. We've got to get it out. Just so we're in sync here, when the next contraction hits, you start pushing. I've delivered animals, but never a baby."

His hand capped her knee for a moment as she caught her breath. When she looked into his eyes, she wished for so many things. Right now, at the top of that list was a healthy baby.

As the contraction came, Kylie rode with it. With all the yearning in her heart, with all the hope in the future she could muster, with all of her past love for Alex and her enduring love for Brock, she pushed and pushed and pushed.

"Looking good," Brock said, concentrating on the baby. "With the next push let's get these shoulders out. Come on, Kylie. Let's do it."

She thought about her child, ready to be born. She thought about Brock's waiting arms and made the most monumental effort of her life to see her baby born.

There were moments of panicked silence, then Brock explained, "I'm cleaning out her mouth."

There was a cry, and he held a baby girl in his hands.

"I want to see her," Kylie murmured, tears flooding down her cheeks.

"You'll see her," Brock said. "I just have to figure out how to do this right."

The feeling in his voice made Kylie look up, right at him. Her breath caught. His expression told her this could be the most important moment of her life.

Chapter Thirteen

The miracle had happened before Brock's eyes.

He was old enough to know life could change in the blink of an eye. It had changed for him the night he had kissed Kylie after her graduation. It had changed when Alex had explained his intentions to marry Kylie. It had changed the moment Brock had set foot in Kylie's hospital room and seen her again after five long years.

Tonight, it had changed most of all. When he'd heard the voice mail message that Kylie had left, he'd wanted to wring her neck. But more than that, he'd wanted to hold her forever. He never wanted her to be in jeopardy. *He* always wanted to keep her safe…to keep her *his*.

At that moment he'd known he could never leave her and had been a fool to think he could. As he'd raced toward town, as he'd called her and learned she was in labor, as he'd heard her telling Molly that her parents loved her even if she were adopted, his heart had begun turning—turning away from the past—turning toward the future... and Kylie...and a child they could raise together.

He loved Kylie Armstrong Warner. Maybe he always had and just hadn't wanted to admit it. He'd been too old, she'd been too young, until the years had evened that out. Now that Alex was gone, why was he continuing to punish himself for being the son that Jack Warner had never wanted? And why did he even care anymore? His life was his to grab onto now.

He'd seen that the moment this child had been born. He'd caught her in his hands and known in his soul that he and Kylie could both give their hearts to this little girl. The love he felt for Kylie and this baby was so powerful it almost brought him to his knees.

He stared at the baby now, mesmerized by her chubby cheeks, her brown hair and her blue eyes. He saw a combination of Kylie's dad and Kylie, Jack and Alex. But most of all, he saw a child who needed two parents—two parents who loved deeply and could commit to each other for the rest of their lives.

Kylie had pulled up her sweater and unclasped her bra. With the umbilical cord still attached, Brock maneuvered the baby onto her stomach, not knowing how to tell her what he was feeling yet sure he had to do it *now.*

Tucking the blanket around the baby, he laid her close to Kylie's breast, asking, "Would you believe me if I told you she's changed everything?"

Kylie's cheeks were wet with tears. "What does that mean?"

The baby quieted as she rooted for Kylie's breast. Finding the nipple, she clasped on.

The sensation made Kylie start…then smile. "I wish you could feel this."

"I do. I feel the bond, Kylie. I know Alex fathered this child, but I want to be a father to her. I want to be a husband to *you*."

When he crouched down beside her, the words poured out. "I love you, Kylie Warner. I've loved you since I first saw your blond hair flying behind you as you rode bareback. You were too young for me to stake a claim. Then I was too late, or too damn considerate to take what I wanted…to think I deserved you. All these weeks I've been telling myself I could leave after this baby was born. I could just walk away. But I can *never* walk away from you, just like I can never walk away from this child." He took Kylie's hand in his and intertwined their fingers.

"Oh, Brock…I'll sell Saddle Ridge," she hurried to say. "We'll start fresh wherever you want to go."

Kneeling beside her, he kissed her fingertips. "You'd actually do that?"

"I love you. I would do *anything* for you, Brock Warner. Absolutely anything."

He knew that now. He knew love was about moving aside anything in the way. He knew love was about forgiveness and healing and looking ahead. "You don't have to *do* anything. I think you've always been able to read me as well as I can read myself, if not better. I *have* always felt connected to Saddle Ridge. And I've always hated loving it because of the way Jack treated me. But you're right. Jack's gone. We can make Saddle Ridge into whatever we want it to be. You and I, together. So…will you marry me?"

Her face was radiant with joy as she held out her arm to him. He bent to kiss her.

They were still kissing when Wanda said from the doorway, "It doesn't look as if you need much help from *me*."

Breaking apart, they both laughed.

"I can take over from here," Wanda assured them. "The paramedics are on their way and, if you'd like, we can have you both checked out at the hospital."

"That sounds like a good idea," Brock decided. Then he looked down at Kylie and put his hand on her shoulder. "But it's your call."

"I'll go to the hospital if you promise to stay by my side."

"Forever," he vowed, and then kissed her again.

Epilogue

One year later

"Reach for the bridle!" Kylie encouraged her one-year-old.

"No, Sarah. Reach for the hammer," Gwen called.

This was a birthday ritual Kylie's dad had told her about when she was a young girl. Parents laid out symbols of career choices on the floor and let their child crawl and reach for the one she preferred. Brock had set out a bridle, a hammer, a twenty-dollar-bill and a doll.

Now Sarah Marie crawled toward all of them quickly as Kylie, Brock, Brock's mother, Gwen, Garrett, Tiffany, Amy, Dylan and Shaye, as well as Molly and her parents, looked on.

All of a sudden Sarah approached the four items, sat before them and grinned at the adults.

"Pick one," Brock encouraged her.

Kylie smiled at her husband. He always encouraged their daughter, praised her as if she were a princess. This little girl had her daddy firmly wound around her finger. Kylie wouldn't have it any other way.

Sarah gave her dad a little wave, turned toward the symbolic items and, at the same time, picked up the bridle in her left hand and the small doll in her right.

Everyone laughed as Brock's mother asked rhetorically, "Why should she have to choose when she can do both like her mom?"

Conchita had been a godsend to Kylie and Brock. Shortly after Sarah's birth, Kylie had asked Brock to invite his mom to attend their wedding and visit with them. She had and, a few months later at their request, she'd moved to Saddle Ridge permanently. She kept all running smoothly so Kylie could concentrate on Sarah and the work she loved. Conchita had even encouraged Kylie and Brock to take the baby to visit Kylie's mom in Colorado during the summer. They had. But Kylie almost felt closer to her mother-in-law now than to her own mother. Brock's mom was a wise woman and the two of them had had many talks about Brock and Saddle Ridge and changing the past into a bright future.

Now Conchita moved to the kitchen where the table was laden with food, including a birthday cake. "Come on, everyone. Dig in."

A few minutes later as all filled their plates and returned to the living room, Molly played with Timmy on the floor near her parents. She'd make a great babysitter in a few years, Kylie thought. Her relationship with her parents was solid again. They'd made the decision together to wait until Molly was sixteen to contact her birth mother. Molly had told Kylie more than once she'd always think of Amanda and George as her *real* parents.

Brock settled Sarah into her high chair beside his armchair. "I remember exactly where I was one year ago tonight."

"It's not a night we'll ever forget." Kylie set a plate with cake in front of their daughter.

Sarah immediately stuck her thumb into it.

Gwen laughed and Garrett hung his arm around her.

"Is it time?" Gwen asked, looking fondly at little Amy sitting in a high chair beside Tiffany.

"It's time," Garrett assured her.

All eyes suddenly focused on Gwen.

"Well, since the gang's all here and this is such a happy occasion, we have an announcement to make."

"You're pregnant!" Shaye erupted with glee as Dylan bounced Timmy on his knee.

"Now how did you guess?" Gwen asked smugly.

When everyone clamored, "We knew it," and "It's about time," Gwen laughed. "I'll be due at the end of August. Can't you all just wait?"

Dylan glanced at Molly and Timmy. "When all of us get together, we'll need a couple of babysitters to keep the kids in line. Just wait until Shaye and I have another one."

"When's that going to happen?" Kylie asked slyly.

"We're discussing it," Shaye said blandly. "And we promise to let you all know just as soon as it happens."

Fondly she glanced over at Tiffany. "Gwen, Kylie and I couldn't be more content. And I heard *you're* taking an accounting course."

"I am. I'll be a bigger help to Garrett if I learn more." Looking shyly at Gwen, she added, "My life's moving along, too." She grinned. "I'm dating somebody."

Garrett scowled. "Yes, and I'm not sure I approve. He's two years older."

"But he wants a career in business management, he's going to school, and you said, yourself, he seems mature. What more could you ask for?"

Garrett looked over at Brock. "Think about Sarah Marie being twenty. What more would *you* ask for?"

"I'd ask for a man to come along who would love her as much as I love her mother," Brock answered surely.

Kylie knew there was no better answer than that.

"She's not going to sleep straight through," Kylie told Brock a few hours later as she undressed in their bedroom. "All that sugar is rolling around inside of her."

He laughed. "It was a great party. I wish Dix would have joined us."

"You know he's shy of crowds. He gets all tongue-tied when there are more than three people in a room. Sarah's going to love his present, as soon as she can fit onto it."

Dix had gotten their daughter a saddle, her very first. "I'm glad he has more time on his hands just to enjoy life now since you've hired more help."

"Yep. That's why he's with friends in town tonight playing poker."

Brock came up behind Kylie, lifted her hair and dragged his finger around the chain on her neck until he came to the mustang dipping between her breasts. "I could get you one of these with diamonds."

She raised her hand and the ring there sparkled. "My engagement ring is big enough. I don't need more diamonds." It was a beautiful, heart-shaped diamond surrounded by a gold, wraparound wedding band that protected it.

Brock rubbed his thumb over the mustang. "I like knowing this is close to your heart, even when I'm not nearby."

Every now and then Brock still took geological consulting work and Kylie didn't mind at all. He loved that work, too. They were building Saddle Ridge up to be more than it had ever been. They had fifteen horses now, a hundred head of Angus. They gentled mustangs, two of which they'd adopted this year, and spent as much time as they could with Sarah Marie.

Kylie turned into Brock's arms. "You've never thought of Sarah as anything but yours, have you?"

"From the moment I held her in my hands, I was her father."

"With all the talk about babies tonight, I was just thinking."

"Thinking? Or planning? One isn't far from the other in *your* head," he claimed with a smile.

"How would you like to be a daddy again?"

Pulling her closer, he asked, "Are we discussing it or are we going to do something about it?"

"I think we should do something about it."

"So do I," he murmured, scooping Kylie up into his arms and carrying her to the bed. As he came down beside her, he said, "I've got to be the happiest man in the world."

"And you've made me the happiest woman."

Kylie kissed her husband, knowing they were going to make another beautiful memory to relive when they turned one hundred and were still fantastically in love.

* * * * *

Set in darkness beyond the ordinary world.
Passionate tales of life and death.
With characters' lives ruled by laws the everyday world
can't begin to imagine.

Introducing NOCTURNE, a spine-tingling new line from
Silhouette Books.

The thrills and chills begin with UNFORGIVEN
by Lindsay McKenna.

Plucked from the depths of hell, former military sharp-shooter Reno Manchahi was hired by the government to kill a thief, but he had a mission of his own. Descended from a family of shape-shifters, Reno vowed to get the revenge he'd thirsted for all these years. But his mission went awry when his target turned out to be a powerful seductress, Magdalena Calen Hernandez, who risked everything to battle a potent evil. Suddenly, Reno had to transform himself into a true hero and fight the enemy that threatened them all. He had to become a Warrior for the Light....

Turn the page for a sneak preview of
UNFORGIVEN
by Lindsay McKenna.
On sale September 26, wherever books are sold.

Chapter 1

One shot...one kill.

The sixteen-pound sledgehammer came down with such fierce power that the granite boulder shattered instantly. A spray of glittering mica exploded into the air and sparkled momentarily around the man who wielded the tool as if it were a weapon. Sweat ran in rivulets down Reno Manchahi's drawn, intense face. Naked from the waist up, the hot July sun beating down on his back, he hefted the sledgehammer skyward once more. Muscles in his thick forearms leaped and biceps bulged. Even his breath was focused on the boulder. In his mind's eye, he pictured Army General Robert Hampton's fleshy, arrogant fifty-year-old features on the rock's surface. Air exploded from between his lips as he brought the avenging hammer down. The boulder pulverized beneath his funneled hatred.

One shot...one kill...

Nostrils flaring, he inhaled the dank, humid heat and drew it deep into his massive lungs. Revenge allowed Reno to endure his imprisonment at a U.S. Navy brig near San Diego, California. Drops of sweat were flung in all directions as the crack of his sledgehammer claimed a third stone victim. Mouth taut, Reno moved to the next boulder.

The other prisoners in the stone yard gave him a wide berth. They always did. They instinctively felt his simmering hatred, the palpable revenge in his cinnamon-colored eyes, was more than skin-deep.

And they whispered he was different.

Reno enjoyed being a loner for good reason. He came from a medicine family of shape-shifters. But even this secret power had not protected him—or his family. His wife, Ilona, and his three-year-old daughter, Sarah, were dead. Murdered by Army General Hampton in their former home on USMC base in Camp Pendleton, California. Bitterness thrummed through Reno as he savagely pushed the toe of his scarred leather boot against several smaller pieces of gray granite that were in his way.

The sun beat down upon Manchahi's naked shoulders, grown dark red over time, shouting his half-Apache heritage. With his straight black hair grazing his thick shoulders, copper skin and broad face with high cheekbones, everyone knew he was Indian. When he'd first arrived at the brig, some of the prisoners taunted him and called him Geronimo. Something strange happened to Reno during his fight with the name-calling prisoners.

Leaning down after he'd won the scuffle, he'd snarled into each of their bloodied faces that if they were going to call him anything, they would call him *gan,* which was the Apache word for *devil.*

His attackers had been shocked by the wounds on their faces, the deep claw marks. Reno recalled doubling his fist as they'd attacked him en masse. In that split second, he'd gone into an altered state of consciousness. In times of danger, he transformed into a jaguar. A deep, growling sound had emitted from his throat as he defended himself in the three-against-one fracas. It all happened so fast that he thought he had imagined it. He'd seen his hands morph into a forearm and paw, claws extended. The slashes left on the three men's faces after the fight told him he'd begun to shape-shift. A fist made bruises and swelling; not four perfect, deep claw marks. Stunned and anxious, he hid the knowledge of what else he was from these prisoners. Reno's only defense was to make all the prisoners so damned scared of him and remain a loner.

Alone. Yeah, he was alone, all right. The steel hammer swept downward with hellish ferocity. As the granite groaned in protest, Reno shut his eyes for just a moment. Sweat dripped off his nose and square chin.

Straightening, he wiped his furrowed, wet brow and looked into the pale blue sky. What got his attention was the startling cry of a red-tailed hawk as it flew over the brig yard. Squinting, he watched the bird. Reno could make out the rust-colored tail on the hawk. As a kid growing up on the Apache reservation in Arizona, Reno knew that all animals that appeared before him were messengers.

Brother, what message do you bring me? Reno knew

one had to ask in order to receive. Allowing the sledgehammer to drop to his side, he concentrated on the hawk who wheeled in tightening circles above him.

Freedom! the hawk cried in return.

Reno shook his head, his black hair moving against his broad, thickset shoulders. *Freedom? No way, Brother. No way.* Figuring that he was making up the hawk's shrill message, Reno turned away. Back to his rocks. Back to picturing Hampton's smug face.

Freedom!

* * * * *

*Look for UNFORGIVEN by Lindsay McKenna,
the spine-tingling launch title from
Silhouette Nocturne™.
Available September 26, wherever books are sold.*

Silhouette®

Desire

THE PART-TIME WIFE

by *USA TODAY* bestselling author

Maureen Child

Abby Talbot was the belle of Eastwick society;
the perfect hostess and wife. If only her
husband were more attentiive. But when
she sets out to teach him a lesson and files
for divorce, Abby quickly learns her husband's
true identity...and exposes them to scandals
and drama galore!

On sale October 2006 from Silhouette Desire!

*Available wherever books are sold,
including most bookstores, supermarkets,
discount stores and drug stores.*

SPECIAL EDITION™

Experience the "magic" of falling in love at Halloween with a new _Holiday Hearts_ story!

UNDER HIS SPELL

by KRISTIN HARDY

October 2006

Bad-boy ski racer J. J. Cooper can get any woman he wants—except Lainie Trask. Lainie's grown up with him and vows that nothing he says or does will change her mind. But J.J.'s got his eye on Lainie, and when he moves into her neighborhood and into her life, she finds herself falling under his spell....

HOLIDAY HEARTS

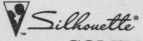

COMING NEXT MONTH

#1783 IT TAKES A FAMILY—Victoria Pade
Northbridge Nuptials
Penniless and raising an infant niece after her sister's death, Karis Pratt's only hope was to go to Northbridge, Montana, and find the baby's father, Luke Walker. Did this small-town cop hold the key to renewed family ties and a bright new future for Karis?

#1784 ROCK-A-BYE RANCHER—Judy Duarte
When rugged Clay Callaghan asked attorney Dani De La Cruz to help bring his orphaned granddaughter back from Mexico, Dani couldn't say no to the case...but what would she say to the smitten cattleman's more personal proposals?

#1785 MOTHER IN TRAINING—Marie Ferrarella
Talk of the Neighborhood
When Zooey Finnegan walked out on her fiancé, the gossips pounced. Unfazed, she went on to work wonders as nanny to widower Jack Lever's two kids. But when she got Jack to come out of his own emotional shell...the town *really* had something to talk about!

#1786 UNDER HIS SPELL—Kristin Hardy
Holiday Hearts
Lainie Trask's longtime crush on J. J. Cooper hadn't amounted to much—J.J. seemed too busy with World Cup skiing and womanizing to notice the feisty curator. But an injury led to big changes for J.J.—including plenty of downtime to discover Lainie's charms....

#1787 LOVE LESSONS—Gina Wilkins
Medical researcher Dr. Catherine Travis had all the trappings of the good life...except for someone special to share it with. Would maintenance man and part-time college student Mike Clancy fix what ailed the good doctor...despite the odds arrayed against them?

#1788 NOT YOUR AVERAGE COWBOY—
Christine Wenger
When rancher Buck Porter invited famous cookbook author and city slicker Merry Turner to help give Rattlesnake Ranch a makeover, it was a recipe for trouble. So what was the secret ingredient that soon made the cowboy, his young daughter and Merry inseparable?